M000119876

Yellow Glass

And Other Ghost Stories

F. K. Young

ST JURMIN

PRESS

© Francis Young 2020

Francis Young has asserted his moral right under the Copyright, Designs and Patents Act, 1988, to be identified as the author of this book.

First published 2020
St Jurmin Press
Peterborough, United Kingdom

A catalogue record for this book is available from the British Library

ISBN 978-0-9926404-8-4

For Tom

Contents

Preface   iv

Yellow Glass   1

This Is My Book   18

Afturganga   27

The Leaven of the Farisees   42

The Ivetot Pedigree   55

The Devil's Breath   67

The Dreamt Book   83

Preface

Historians have long had a special relationship with the writing of ghost stories. Some even speak of the 'antiquarian ghost story' as a subgenre written by, or as if by, scholars of the past. The work of the historian often feels like communing with the dead, and dwelling in the historical imagination can render the past more real than the present for the unwary scholar. Yet even the greatest historical imagination is just that – a feel for the imagined past based upon intense study of the sources that is, nonetheless, separated as if by the veil of time from *the past in itself*. That true past, the ultimately unrecoverable lived experience of the dead, is the ghost encountered by every historian. It is able to speak, sometimes at length, but it is not of our world; it cannot abide on this plane of existence.

The historian is a kind of necromancer. As the seventeenth-century antiquary John Aubrey wrote, "The retrieving of these forgotten things from oblivion in some sort resembles the Art of a Conjuror who makes those walke and appeare that have layen in their graves many hundreds of yeares." Scholars of the past dwell among the dead, and it is perhaps for this reason that several historians and antiquaries have been drawn to the writing of ghost stories as a means of expressing what the writing of history may not articulate, at least not in any direct way: that there is something uncanny in drawing so close to the past.

Readers are often interested in whether writers of ghost stories believe in ghosts. For historians, archaeologists, archivists and others who live among the detritus of the past, that may seem the wrong question to ask. Ghosts are surely encountered, whether we believe in them or not; there are moments when the imagined past takes on a kind of independent life, or half-life – whether in the handling of an object, the reading of a manuscript, or in the whispering spaces of buildings and ruins. Becoming aware of this stirring life can be as unnerving as the appearance of any Gothic spectre rattling chains. It is no wonder, to me at least, that writing ghost stories is a pursuit of antiquaries.

I grew up in the same landscape as M. R. James, whom many consider to be the greatest of all ghost story writers: the eerie transition from chalk uplands to sandy Breckland just north of the Suffolk town of Bury St Edmunds; and, like James, I was captivated from an early age by the Cyclopean ruins of the vast medieval Abbey of St Edmund at the heart of the town. I followed in James's footsteps to the University of Cambridge, and became like him a historian of that great Abbey of St Edmund, and of the ecclesiastical antiquities of the county of Suffolk. Again and again, I find myself returning to James's indispensable antiquarian work on my home county. And like that great antiquary, I am drawn to trying to understand the strangeness of what people believed in the past.

It would be ambitious and presumptuous of me to hope that the quality of my scholarship ever matches that of M. R. James, let alone the quality of my fiction. I draw the comparison only to show that antiquaries often find themselves treading similar paths, especially if they originate from the same place and grow up with similar experiences of the past. James himself felt a strong affinity with the seventeenth- and eighteenth-century scholars of the antiquities of Suffolk, such as John Battely and Thomas Martin of Palgrave. This is another way in which the scholar of the past communes with ghosts; they are part of a community of enquiry that includes both the living and the dead. In many cases, the manuscript collections of antiquaries remain unpublished – so there are still new conversations to be had with them, centuries after their deaths; they are still to be engaged with, challenged, and honoured for their pioneering achievements.

The ghost story can, therefore, be a product of antiquarian pursuits. It is certainly not an inevitable product – but it does manifest itself with striking frequency. I believe this is because the ghost story, as a literary form, gives the historian a means of writing about the experience of living with the past – the experience that gives rise to works of historical scholarship, but is not itself directly expressible in them.

I would not have thought of collecting any of my ghost stories for publication if it had not been for a pleasant surprise I received in December 2018. The story 'This Is My Book' (included in this collection), which I had idly entered in a ghost story competition ('Ghosts in the Bookshop') run by The Petersfield Bookshop and judged by Michelle Magorian, was the recipient of a runner-up prize. Up to that point, although I had occasionally penned ghost stories for circulation among friends, I had not thought anyone might consider them worthy of publication. However, like many a scholar before me, wisely or not, I have given in to the lure of the antiquarian ghost story.

I am grateful to those who have been kind enough to read and comment on these stories, especially Roger Clarke, and I thank Lauren Dartnell for her kind permission to use her photograph of stained glass at Great Walsingham, Norfolk in the front cover design.

Serpentine Green, Peterborough
September 2020

Yellow Glass

Ilse was not altogether surprised she had not heard of Saint-Hamond; there were, after all, so many little towns in the South of France with big, mutilated churches, once the cathedrals of tiny dioceses before the Revolution. Not many of them were renowned for their stained glass, and Ilse usually ended up working on the famous cathedrals of the north – albeit she still hankered for the chance to work at Chartres, the dream of every stained glass conservator. The request from the Commune of Saint-Hamond appealed to her, however; she had never worked in that part of France before. The partnership's lead conservator determined that Ilse should go alone at first to survey the window; her colleague Kristian would join her only once she had determined the extent of the repairs required. The job was a single window, reportedly not a very large one, and a major project for the team was looming at Rouen.

While the appeal for help came from the Commune, it was down to the clergy of the ex-cathedral to host Ilse for the duration of the project. She arrived in Saint-Hamond on an intensely hot Sunday afternoon; even the dry breeze was a relief from the bus's broken air conditioning. She went straight to the address the Curé had given her, getting her first look at the cathedral as she crossed the town's sun-scorched main square. It was an unlovely and haphazard architectural compilation of multiple eras of rebuilding: Romanesque in origin, heavily ornamented and rebuilt in the *Grand Siècle*, then brutally truncated after the Revolution. It was easy to see why this church did not make it into the pages of guides to France's cathedrals. The only remaining portion of the west tower was an unattractive stump, while the façade was a mess; the decaying Romanesque narthex (often the redeeming feature of such buildings) had been largely pulled down in the nineteenth century, leaving behind the gouged-out ghosts of Romanesque sculpture. Above it all was an odd rose window; Romanesque originally, perhaps, but now filled with heavy seventeenth-century tracery.

As a professional conservator, Ilse found every building with stained glass interesting – it was the uniqueness of the technical challenge, rather than features of a building that might appeal to tourists, that made her work memorable and rewarding. For now, though, she was relieved to step out of the sunbaked cathedral square into the cool shade of the Rue des Chanoines, a narrow lane leading up to the maze of medieval streets on the site of the old Roman town. Her first impressions of Saint-Hamond were unpromising; the place was none too clean, with an obvious stray dog problem, and Ilse was fairly sure those were little rivulets of canine urine in the gutters of the Rue des Chanoines. The yelling of adults, children and infants drifted from open windows high above the street, where discoloured and billowing net curtains almost touched their counterparts on the other side of the lane.

Number 30 was marked very officially with white digits on a blue enamel plaque, but the building was in an advanced state of decay. Greenery sprouted from cracks in the tainted rendering, and the great wooden gate looked as though it might cave in at any moment. Ilse yanked at a great bell pull like an iron poker. After a long wait, the gate shuddered and she heard the drawing back of bolts. At first, she feared she might have the wrong house; the woman who appeared did not look much like the custodian of a *maison paroissiale*.

"What?" the woman demanded.

"I'm the stained glass conservator. I'm supposed to meet Fr Etienne?"

"Etienne's not here." She began closing the gate.

Ilse moved forward slightly. "I'm supposed to be staying here, I think."

"Lucky you." The woman stood aside to allow Ilse into the courtyard that lay beyond the decaying gate.

"I've got Fr Etienne's number somewhere…" Ilse reached for her phone, but the woman was already disappearing back through a dark doorway on one side of a cobbled courtyard overgrown with long, bleached grass.

The Curé was there within minutes. He was a short, balding man with intense black hair and leathery, olive-hued skin. He must have been nearing sixty, Ilse thought, but he had a youthful and kind face.

"So Madeleine let you in? She can be a little… rough. I apologise. We let her stay here, and do the odd job around the church. She's had a troubled life. Let me take your bag!"

The priest shouldered Ilse's rucksack and mounted a set of creaking wooden stairs in the opposite wing to Madeleine's.

"We're so grateful you could come. It's decades since anyone has dealt properly with *La Rosace Jaune.*"

"That's the window? The yellow rose, you call it?"

"Yes! It's very yellow, as you'll see. A remarkable window. You haven't brought much with you!" the priest remarked, as he set her rucksack down on the dusty floor.

"No; I'm doing the survey first; my colleague Kristian will be driving down from Cologne with the tools we'll need."

"Ah! I see. How long will the survey take, do you think?"

"Just a couple of days. By the end of tomorrow I should be able to let Kristian know exactly what we need."

The priest nodded. "That's great, great! Well, you mustn't do anything this afternoon – just get settled in and take a look around. We'll go to the cathedral tomorrow. But I insist you have dinner at the *doyenné.*"

*

The deanery, just off the cathedral square, was less grand than its name suggested; once again, Ilse suspected it had been much truncated in the nineteenth century, but it remained a characterful old house of heavy, pockmarked limestone blocks. The Curé received the conservator warmly in a small panelled library, pressing an aperitif into her hand.

"I'm afraid it's not really much of a cathedral," he remarked apologetically. "Not really a cathedral at all. You must have worked on much grander places."

"Bigger ones, certainly. But I'm interested to see what Saint-Hamond has to offer."

4

Fr Etienne gave a short laugh. "Well, it's certainly unique!"

"How, exactly?"

"Well – I know I said you shouldn't start at the cathedral until tomorrow, but it really is best if I show you. Don't treat this as work, though!"

It was a bright summer evening, ideal for viewing stained glass – albeit not, perhaps, a window that faced due west. Ilse followed the Curé into his overgrown garden, which backed directly onto the shapeless north flank of the cathedral's once great nave. Drawing out a heavy set of keys, he unlocked a pale blue door that admitted them to the church. The scent of dust and cheap candlewax enveloped the two small figures as they crossed a nave floor speckled with coloured light from Belle Époque clerestory windows of little merit. The Curé unlocked another narrow door into what remained of the west tower, a cavernous and filthy space filled with bird and bat droppings where a single, crude wooden stairway led up to the organ loft. Ilse's hands were stained black with the dust of the treads by the time she reached the platform.

Moving behind the huge mass of the eighteenth-century organ, Ilse was suddenly confronted by the *rosace*; huge, of course, at this proximity. Her first impression was of the overpowering *yellowness* of that glass; at this time of day, when the sun was setting directly behind the west window, it was almost blinding. Gradually, however, Ilse's eyes adjusted. She had seen many rose windows, but this one was surely the strangest. The glass was clearly of seventeenth-century date, as was the tracery, but instead of imitating the leaf-like patterns of high medieval decorated architecture, this tracery had a distinctly geometrical look. The 'rose' had the appearance of an elaborate star – or even a snowflake – divided into triangular, rhomboid or diamond-shaped compartments by the thick stone tracery.

Stranger than the structure of the window was the manner of its decoration. Ilse was not especially surprised to see some grotesque demons at the bottom of the window, but as she cast her eyes over the whole piece she saw nothing other than the grinning, hairy faces of fallen angels, rendered in an unusually rich array of colours with a startling degree of imagination. Only at the centre of the rose was there something different – what looked like Hebrew letters in a plain circle. It was the colour yellow, however, that predominated; far from suffering divine punishment, the demons rolled, frolicked and swam in a flood of yellow hues, from pale lemon to dark mustard. From the first, Ilse found the window repellent. She did not usually leap to such firmly held judgements about the effect a work of art had on her; but something about this thing produced strong feelings of disgust.

"It's very… unusual," she ventured to Etienne.

He smiled, and nodded. "You can see why they built a great big organ in front of it, eh?"

"That's not altogether unusual for a west window…"

"It's the oldest glass in the church, though that's not saying much. But the Commune wants it preserved for posterity. I suppose they want the tourists to come for the stories about it."

"Stories? What stories?"

The priest laughed. "Come! Let's head back to our dinner and I'll tell you all about it."

*

They spoke no more of the window until Etienne had cleared away the remains of the crêpes and Chantilly. Pouring Ilse another glass of wine, he asked her,

"So, do you want to know what they say about that thrice-damned window?"

"I thought you'd never ask!"

The Curé sat back and brought the fingers of both hands together into an arch. "It was a Canon Lecouturier who made it, we think in about 1674. He was apprenticed to a glazier before he went to the seminary, so he knew the craft – or some of it, at least. Of course, he didn't make the thing singlehandedly, but he certainly directed it pretty closely. This Lecouturier – he gained himself an unsavoury reputation. It wasn't a bright time for the church back then. There was a lot of ambition, a lot of hunger for power, a lot of superstition. You must have heard what happened in Paris – the poisonings, the sacrilegious rites, the awful tortures, the executions. That was the court of the Sun King!" he scoffed. "But it infected the provinces too; the priests were rotten, especially in the cathedrals. The bishop was the fifth son of some nobleman, always in Paris, never around; and they say Lecouturier poisoned the dean in the hope of taking his place.

"At least the chapter never gave Lecouturier the top job; but Lecouturier was in charge anyway. He lived here, in this very house," Etienne glanced around him. "It makes me shiver sometimes… They say he gave himself up to Satan; the income from his canonry wasn't enough for the life he wanted – for the wine, the dining, the women; so he wrote a book of the black art and conjured Beelzebub himself."

7

"Of course he did...!" Ilse smiled. "It's a great story, go on."

Etienne was smiling too, albeit a little more nervously. He continued.

"The citizens of Saint-Hamond – they hated this man. Despised him utterly. They wanted him dead. A few even tried. But everyone feared Lecouturier's book. They knew what he was capable of.

"Anyway, when he controlled the cathedral's finances, the canon brought in the glaziers to put in that west window. They worked under very strict instructions; and they say the old canon painted those horrors himself. There's a guidebook that says the window is the name of God driving away the demons of hell."

"Yes; that makes sense, I think."

Etienne nodded. "You'd think so. But the name of God in Hebrew – the Tetragrammaton – it's not hard to recognise. Whatever that is in the middle of the window, it's not Hebrew, and it's not the Tetragrammaton."

"Blundered by an artist who didn't know the language. It's not uncommon."

"Perhaps. Anyway, old Lecouturier died. Naturally, apparently. And after his death the citizens broke into this house, and they found that black book of his and brought it out into the cathedral square. They built a bonfire and burnt it." Etienne leant forward over the table, and lowered his voice slightly. "But just as they thought the old canon was gone, and his power was nullified – one of the men caught sight of a page of that book as it shrivelled in the fire. It was a figure to summon the powers of hell, and he recognised it as the window above them. Old Lecouturier got the last laugh – he'd made his book part of the cathedral itself. Well, after that the burgesses tried to get the window taken out.

But stained glass is expensive. Lecouturier was dead and gone, and the dean and the bishop wouldn't listen to the citizens' wild tales. And after a while the canons shoved a great big organ in front of it anyway, so you could barely see it. But they say Lecouturier has never really left the cathedral – that he made that window to tie his spirit to the place." The Curé raised his glass. "Anyway, that's the story!"

Ilse could not deny that the legend discomforted her. "I suppose there's always a grain of truth in these stories, isn't there? The canon was unpopular; unpopular people get accused of all sorts of things. I suppose he just had odd tastes. What do you think – as a priest, I mean?"

"As a priest?" Etienne laughed. "As a priest, I get on with my job. The Commune wants that window repaired. I don't own the church, do I? It's not my choice. If it were up to me … I'm not sure I wouldn't just leave that glass to fall out."

*

Ilse was kept awake for much of the night. Madeleine had been screaming at someone, slamming doors, and throwing things; at one point Ilse was sure two people were running past her door, yelling French expletives at the tops of their voices. When she did sleep, her dreams were not pleasant. She was leaving the *maison paroissiale* and walking down to the deserted cathedral square; as she turned to look up at the cathedral, that devilish window was suddenly lit from within by an unnatural glow. There was a presence; someone behind her, a powerful sense of malevolence – and then she woke in the early dawn, feeling groggy and unsettled. An early cup of coffee in the upper town was

9

swiftly followed by a second; then Ilse felt more or less ready to face the day.

She knew Etienne was saying mass at eight o'clock, so she slipped into the back of a tiny congregation of half a dozen elderly women. She rarely went to church in Germany, but she found the liturgy soothing, and Etienne was a reassuring presence. She sat there for a long time at the end of the service, waiting while Etienne dealt with his garrulous parishioners, until the priest finally returned from the back of the church.

"You're very patient, Ilse. And early!" he exclaimed. "Did you want to join me for some breakfast?"

Ilse did not feel like eating. Making her excuses, she took the key to the organ loft from the Curé.

"Well ... I'll leave you to it."

The cathedral was open to the public, but Ilse did not think a single human being came into the building throughout that whole morning. She set up her laptop and began photographing the window; morning was the best time to do so, of course, when the sun was not shining directly through the rose. Her first impression of the glass remained unchanged. There was something about the gleefulness of the demons that sat uneasily with their presence in a church. Whoever painted these surely had a disturbed imagination. The lifelike devils displayed extraordinary variety, sporting a mixture of animal and insect body parts, bloated bellies and hairy heads, goat-like hooves, scorpion-like stings, bulging eyes, pig-like snouts – and always gaping mouths with a laughing expression. Instead of the blacks, reds and browns usually used to portray the denizens of hell, these fallen angels were of all hues. There was something faintly blasphemous in colouring these monstrosities with rich blues more commonly seen on the robe of the Virgin. The technical skill of the glass painter was undeniable; his taste, debateable.

Ilse steadily worked her way around the window with her camera. What she really needed was a stepladder, or a drone – Kristian would bring one of those, to ensure they could properly inspect the uppermost reaches of the window. The *rosace* was clearly in poor shape; the stone tracery was crumbling, probably from water damage originally let in through the roof, and made worse when the glass started buckling, creating more gaps for moisture. The glass bulged inwards in several places, outwards in others, and the leading was in a poor state indeed. As it moved closer to noon, Ilse found herself increasingly dazzled by that overpowering yellow. The entire organ loft was flooded with a sickly, mustard light. As the sun rose high in the sky, the polychrome shadows of the window's unattractive occupants began to appear on the dusty boards beneath Ilse's feet, and dappled her bare arms as she struggled to see the screen of her laptop. She could hardly work here, she reasoned; as she turned once more to look at the window it seemed as though it were gently rotating, and the figures moving – clearly an effect of too much intense con-centration on the glass. She needed to take a break.

She packed up and began descending the stairs. It was a lovely relief to her eyes to pass into the dark void of the west tower; but about halfway down the steps, when she was still looking up at the organ loft, she was certain she saw a dark shadow move across the bright colours speckling the north side of the church, as if someone were moving up there – impossible, of course, since she had been alone in the organ loft all morning. Clearly, she reasoned, her senses were more addled by the yellow light than she thought.

The afternoon's task was inspecting the window from the outside. Enough remained of the demolished narthex to make it possible to walk in front of the *rosace* along a narrow gallery, although Ilse was still unsure how she would get onto the gallery when she called Etienne on her mobile.

"I'll come over with the key at three," he said. "And you shouldn't go up there alone – it's pretty narrow."

At a dismal little restaurant with flimsy plastic tables, Ilse managed to find sufficient Wi Fi to email some of the photos to Kristian. Etienne met her outside the cathedral at three, brandishing his huge set of keys.

"I don't often get to use this one," he said, separating a short silver key from the rest.

Access to the outer gallery, it turned out, was not from the organ loft but through a tiny door Ilse had hitherto overlooked inside the void of the west tower; low, grime-blackened and almost rotten, it led into an even smaller turret barely visible from the exterior. A set of two uninviting ladders, almost vertical, gave access to a trapdoor which Etienne forced open; it was not locked. Daylight and the noise of the square flooded suddenly in upon them and Ilse and the Curé stepped gingerly onto a narrow leaded void between the upper west front of the church and the remains of the Romanesque narthex roof. There was no handrail as such, but what remained of the narthex gave at least some protection from falling. Ahead of them lay the massive, stained stone tracery of the *rosace jaune*. From this side, of course, the yellowness of the glass was much harder to recognise, and the mirror-image demons grinned obscurely from dark depths. Ilse reached for the camera around her neck and began taking photographs. The damage was much clearer to see on this side. She had seen this many times before; under the acidic grime of the town below, the stonework was turning to sand, flaking away in long crumbling fingers.

"You know you need a stonemason here, not a glass expert?" Ilse remarked to the Curé, who nodded. "I've told the Commune. You're cheaper, apparently."

"The fact is, there's not a lot I can do to secure the glass from further damage if the stone tracery is this unstable. I mean, I can survey it and tell you what needs doing…"

Ilse leant in to examine one part of the window, where a broad diamond of glass was pulling away from the tracery completely.

"Ha! You can see right inside through this one. This might be where a lot of your water dam– "

Mid-sentence, Ilse was robbed of the capacity to speak. Where before she had seen only void space, as she looked back into the crevice between stone and leading, a *human eye* was momentarily there; wide open, like the eyes of a person suffering a seizure; the pupil intensely black, and the whites – if they could be called that – a sickly shade of yellow. And there was an accompanying smell; a stench, unmistakable, of human decay.

She staggered back; Etienne, mercifully, managed to catch her before she backed into the edge of the gallery. He did not see the eye; but he did catch the overpowering smell.

"My God! What is that?"

Ilse summoned all her strength to keep her voice as level as possible. "I'd like to go down now, please."

Etienne saw immediately how white she had gone. "Of course, of course." He ushered her back to the trapdoor. "It's OK. Come back to the *doyenné*, please."

13

They passed quickly through the body of the church and through the side door into the Curé's garden. Ilse felt immense relief as they left the building, although her entire body felt tense, with cold shivers running over her limbs like the onset of illness.

"You saw something, didn't you?" Said the priest, as he guided Ilse to a chair. "You don't have to tell me if you don't want to. But I think you should. Drink?"

"Just water, thank you."

He brought back a tall glass from the kitchen. Ilse's voice broke as she tried to describe what she had seen.

"Who the hell was in there? Who the hell would try to scare me like that? And what was that *smell*?"

"I don't know what you believe in, Ilse," the priest said slowly, "but I don't think this was something ... natural."

Ilse thought of that strange shadow she had seen moving in the organ loft that morning, when she knew no-one was up there.

"I don't normally ... I mean I wouldn't usually believe..."

"It's not really about belief when we come up against it, is it? I know you don't like that window; you sensed something about it the first time you saw it up close."

"It's true; I don't like it. I should be more objective as a conservator..."

"You're not being a conservator right now, Ilse. You've had a shock and we need to think about what we can do."

"I'm not sure I can face going up there again, if I'm honest." Ilse put her head in her hands; it felt like a professional failure.

"There may be something we can do."

Ilse looked up. "What?"

The priest sat down opposite her. "Do you know what has always struck me about that story – the story about the canon I told you last night? It's the hate. Lecouturier hated the *Saint-Hamondois*; the *Saint-Hamondois* hated him. When he died, when they burnt that book, it was a response of *hate*. I wonder what a response of love could do."

"What do you mean, a response of love?"

"I could pray for him. You could, too, if you want to."

Ilse scoffed. "He's been dead three hundred years…!"

"Dead, yes. But are you going to tell me he isn't somehow still here?"

She shook her head. "I can't think about that. God! It's too horrible."

"Could you bear to go into that organ loft one more time?" the Curé asked. "Don't worry, I'll be with you right the way through. But I need your help with something. I think it's worth trying; I don't think it's ever been done before."

*

Reluctantly, Ilse agreed to meet Etienne in the organ loft at six o'clock the next morning, well before the morning mass. As she left the *doyenné* she did not dare even glance at that rose window; and the second night in the *maison paroissiale* was more horrible than the first. Madeleine and her boyfriend, or whoever he was, resumed the banging of doors – but Ilse was more disturbed by her dreams than by any outside noises. A jumble of images assembled and disassembled in her mind's eye, always with that yellow glass at the centre of it. The demons came alive, circling and chasing their tails like vile pathogens caught in the glare of a microscope; and then the entire *rosace* began to rotate, like an infernal machine for the production of horror, the unknown letters of that central inscription glowing white hot as the denizens of the glass began to take three-dimensional form. Pulling their swollen bodies from the viscous glass, like insects escaping amber, they swarmed out of their prison like locusts into the town of Saint-Hamond, taking Canon Lecouturier's revenge on the inhabitants. And in the centre of the town square, holding up his accursed book with pallid hands, stood a black-cloaked figure – conducting them like an orchestra, sending them forth as his servants to do unutterable evil. Then, as the window span, it was turning into something else – a huge eye, its whites putrid yellow, and an all-seeing pupil flickered from side to side before fixing its gaze on Ilse.

Ilse awoke feeling drained of life and energy – but she hurried past the early deliveries of fruit and bread to her rendezvous at the cathedral. Even after such a short time, she felt she trusted Etienne; if anyone could do something about this, perhaps he could. She found him in the organ loft, as he had said; a flimsy table, where yesterday she had rested her laptop, was drawn up in front of the *rosace*. On it the priest had placed a white cloth and the essentials for mass.

"Are you still happy to do this?" the Curé asked. "It's important that you pray for him – however you might feel. You were the one who saw him. He showed himself to you, for some reason. I hope it was for this reason."

"I don't think I'm much good at praying…"

Etienne shook his head. "I think you know what to do. Put him in God's care. If I'm right, then that's all he is asking for."

The priest lifted a thin violet stole over his head and began a mass for the departed. Ilse tried to fix her eyes on Etienne, but her gaze was involuntarily drawn to the loathsome glass; and whether it was a trick of the light or not, as the priest prayed, the peculiar inscription in an unknown alphabet at the centre of the *rosace jaune* seemed to grow fainter. At the words of consecration, it looked as if it disappeared altogether. Etienne, who was facing Ilse, did not see the effect. But when the mass was over, they both looked closely at the glass. Etienne even reached up and touched it. There could be no doubt; at the centre of the rose window was a circle of plain yellow glass.

This Is My Book

Bournegate Books was a bookshop in the terminal phase of its existence. The chamber of commerce wondered how Roger had kept it going for so long. The building itself was nice enough – an eye-catching Tudor stone cottage a few houses up from the lovely medieval bridge. It would have made a perfect teashop. But the flaking hand-painted sign, last retouched in the mid-nineties, its widening cracks and grooves filled with black grime, was hardly inviting. The bulging oriel window at the front of the shop was filthy inside and out; a small mercy, given the state of Roger's window displays. No-one could remember when he had last changed the sorry, sun-bleached and curling collection of books that was unfortunate enough to advertise what lay inside.

The shop's interior embarrassed the handful of customers who crossed the threshold. Most people were too polite to turn round and head straight back out onto Bournegate, instead making a feigned circuit of the first room. They tried to avoid tripping over the piles of books encroaching on a soiled green carpet, worn skin-thin and shiny by decades of shoes. Anyone who took the trouble to inspect the stock found a mixture of buckled yellowing paperback novels (the kind that someone once tried to read on a train before casting it aside half unread), multi-volume sets for display, never opened – usually Dickens or Reader's Digests – and thick hardback biographies of forgotten celebrities with garish, plasticised dust jackets adorned with gold letters. Every shelf was full, wedged in with books above and below, while unruly piles grew steadily from the floor like stalagmites. Given the immense number of books in the shop, the most dedicated searchers – the kind of people who cannot pass a bookshop without entering it – emerged astounded that there was not a single volume worth reading.

In truth, Bournegate Books was not so much a shop as a storeroom of raw materials. The real source of the meagre income that kept the shop open was Roger's back room, a dingy Georgian brick annexe to the Tudor building that was a bibliophile's house of horrors. Every afternoon after closing, Roger retreated to the back room, switched on a machine saw and attacked a pile of books bound together with industrial glue, separating the spines and an inch-long section of pages from the rest of the books. Using more glue, Roger then fixed these mutilated remnants of literature to a plank of MDF, the length cut according to his client's specifications. There was a lot of demand from renovated pubs and restaurants for these *trompe l'oeil* bookshelves, especially where there was no room to have the depth of an actual bookshelf. If a client wanted to decorate using unmutilated books, Roger could supply those as well, selecting books according to colour, size or general appearance. Letting nothing go to waste, Roger used the leftover parts of the decapitated books as kindling for the wood-burning stove that kept him warm while he worked.

Big paperbacks burnt the best, as if the unctuous words of bestseller-writers oozed out of fat blocks of turgid prose to feed the flames. Getting rid of the detritus of hardbacks was an annoyance. The plasticated dust jackets gave off unpleasant fumes when burnt, while the boards were rarely incinerated completely, leaving large fragments in the grate. All in all, however, Roger found books an economical alternative to wood; a good-sized Barbara Cartland would easily smoulder for an hour, and was as good as a small log.

Roger could not remember the last time he had opened a book, beyond scrutinising the boards and endpapers for the all-important pencilled price, or to check the book's title, publisher and edition if he thought it might be worth selling online. Yet even Roger's online sales had dried up recently; he found he lacked the patience to track down individual books and calculate an asking price. Increasingly, Roger consigned the more interesting volumes to a local auction house and took a nominal fee. Few booksellers could clear a house-full of books as quickly as Roger could, and his reputation with the auction houses was built on his speed and willingness to take on any job.

Clearing a hoarder's house, without doubt, was the best opportunity to shift books at scale. Roger always kept an ear out for a dead hoarder. So he was one of the first on the scene when Shabby Annie finally expired from a combination of cheap whisky, old age and the November cold. She had been a familiar figure in the town for as long as Roger had lived there, shuffling along the pavements in all weathers, wrapped in layers of ancient and malodorous winter coats. She always pushed a contraption – presumably of her own devising – composed of the skeleton of an old pram and capacious, filthy bicycle panniers.

Judging from her appearance, most people assumed Shabby Annie was homeless, but Roger knew better. Several times he had seen her cramming her push-along into a narrow Victorian building behind the Chinese takeaway on River Lane. When he heard from the manager of the charity shop a few doors up Bournegate that Annie was no more, a couple of calls put Roger in touch with the building's landlord, who was only too willing to let Roger clear out any books he could find before the industrial cleaners went in, and even offered him fifty pounds for the job.

Roger had been in some unsanitary homes before – and, as the state of his own bookshop testified, he was no stranger to chaos – yet the former home of Shabby Annie shocked even the bookseller. Annie had hoarded everything, living and dead – but, above all, she had hoarded books. The three squalid rooms she had somehow managed to live in were not so much piled as inundated with a tide of print – wave upon wave of dismal paperbacks, with burrows and nests of paper here and there where Annie's cats (long since taken away by the RSPCA) and other less savoury creatures had gnawed and pawed themselves comfortable niches in the literary avalanche.

That night, with rubber gloves, heavy-duty bin liners, a wheelbarrow and a small van, Roger sweated his way through the old woman's monstrous book hoard. He barely had time to glance at the titles, although he gathered that Annie's major period of collecting had been the 1970s, with a preference for cheap pulpy books about spiritualism, black magic, witchcraft, astrology and any other nonsense she could lay her hands on. He certainly had no time to open any of the books, but the damage done by felines and rodents meant that some of them were missing their covers. It was for this reason that Roger's glance fell on some writing inside one of the books. There were four lines written with a blue ballpoint pen, in a crabbed and wavering hand that Roger thought could only be Annie's:

I curse you thief who this book took
My curse on him who mars this book
This is my book I shall not part
With this my book by any art

Out of curiosity, Roger glanced at a couple of other books, and then a couple more; to his surprise, Annie seemed to have taken the trouble to write the same lines of doggerel in every one. It seemed odd, to say the least, that a woman with so little respect for books had bothered to inscribe them all. The bookseller chuckled to himself. Curse or not, the vast majority of Annie's collection was destined for Roger's wood-burning (or more properly book-burning) stove. Most of the books – creased, mildewed or gnawed by rats and mice – were unsellable in any form.

Roger did not want to waste any time in getting rid of the book-filled bin liners that were clogging up his shop. That night, he pulled some of the volumes less affected by damp out of the nearest bag and threw them into the stove. They would not catch fire at first – clearly the pervasive damp of Annie's quarters had penetrated the pages more deeply than Roger had thought. But at long last, with the help of some firelighters, the yellow pages slowly began to smoulder.

It was already ten o'clock, and Roger still had a long night ahead of him. There was a nice Regency volume of county excursions on his workbench whose engravings needed to be cut out, slotted in plastic wallets and priced before the rejected pages went into the furnace. The old, rag-bound paper always burnt nicely. Tonight, the heat of the stove barely cut through the moist cold of the advancing winter. Roger reached to put the radio on, but the battery was dead. Another armful of Annie's books went into the furnace. He watched them for a moment, tongues of flame licking printed pentacles and zodiacs for a moment before curling them into oblivion. He caught a glimpse of another of those shaky yet purposeful inscriptions. Roger was surprised that, even with his face next to the open stove, he was still shivering.

He returned to his work. It must have been at least an hour later that he noticed something – a light glimpsed over the top of his reading glasses where it should not have been. He looked up. The door between the annexe and the main part of the shop was open. It was a light in the bookshop. Roger groaned with annoyance that he had left something on, even though the light was an unusual colour – a sort of blue glow rather than the cheerful yellow glow of a bulb. Whatever it was, Roger felt obliged to heave himself up from the bench and make his way into the shop.

The bookseller cursed loudly when he reached behind the door and flicked the light switch, only to find the piles of books still in darkness. The annexe and shop were on separate circuits, and he had wondered for a while if the shop's wiring was close to failure. But it was a minor setback; the bulb in the annexe gave some light, and Roger knew the layout of his shop and the positions of the treacherous book piles well enough to navigate it in semi-darkness. The blue glow he had seen from the annexe had seemingly vanished; the front part of the shop was mantled by a thick silence that took Roger aback. There was no double-glazing in the ancient windows fronting Bournegate, and the sounds of the street normally trickled in even at this late hour. It was an oppressive, unwelcome silence that confronted Roger with the disquieting sounds of his own body. There were street lamps outside, but the shop seemed somehow to be darkening from within. Roger heard himself breathing more shallowly.

The next thing he heard did not come from himself; it was a rustle and a thud in the shop's basement. Despairing of the number of bin bags full of Annie's books, Roger had thrown some of them down the steep stairs. Unsurprisingly for this part of town, the cellar was older even than the shop above it. Down there, the curious creatures of a medieval stonemason's fevered imagination, bearing up groined arches on their backs, grinned out into an almost perpetual blackness. Roger was not a superstitious man, but he had to admit to himself that he did not much like that cellar, and avoided going down there. The sounds of movement in the cellar continued. The cause was obvious – so close to the river, he had dealt with rats in the cellar before. Then a more revolting thought crossed his mind – that some living creature from Shabby Annie's flat had somehow hitched a ride in one of the bags. In any case, there was nothing to be done about a possible infestation until the morning.

As he turned to go, Roger was unable to shake the burden of instinct, which told him – against all reason – that whatever was moving and rustling in that cellar was a lot bigger than any rat. When he heard what was unmistakably a footfall on the steps, a few seconds passed in which Roger felt himself disengage from reality – before a sudden rush of blood to his heart told him that what he was experiencing was real. There was no way into the building from the cellar – not in modern times, anyway. But why would a burglar even bother with his shop, and why visit the cellar? Roger backed towards the till; he saw no sign of it being tampered with, although the blue glow he had seen was presumably the light of the burglar's torch.

Clearly there was no time to call the police; he had left his mobile in the annexe. The footfalls were approaching the top of the stairs now, close to the shop's till. Roger's eyes had adjusted to the near darkness, and he looked desperately around for some object he might defend himself with. He remembered, with a twinge of panic, the old jeweller on Priory Road who was found with his head smashed in with a crowbar in the flat above his shop. Roger grabbed the only remotely defensive object within reach, an ancient golfing umbrella behind his threadbare chair, and readied himself to brandish it as threateningly as he could.

The burglar should be at the top of the stairs by now, but he seemed to have stopped; Roger saw no-one framed in the door to the cellar stairs. In fact, he saw nothing at all; the dim patch of stone his eyes had been focussed on seemed to have slipped into darkness.

And then he understood, and as he did so his grip tightened around the umbrella so that the metal struts dug into his fingers. The darkness itself was advancing from the cellar; a sentient, groping darkness that, he now realised, carried with it an unmistakable smell. A stench of cheap whisky and long-unwashed wool.

Roger was backing out from behind the counter and into the body of the shop. He thrust a hand into his pocket – thank God, he still had his keys. Roger launched himself towards the warm streetlights of Bournegate and the shop's front door. He tried to fit the right key to the lock; but, try as he might, his hands were trembling too much. It was too late. Roger thought of the loose sash window on the first floor; the darkness had not yet closed off the way to the stairs. But as he ran it reached him, and he was enveloped in its soft, obscene embrace. Before he tripped and fell, Roger heard the rhythm of words hissed without human lips.

This is my book, I shall not part
With this my book by any art …

*

"I always told him that shop was a death trap," the manager of the charity shop observed to one of his regular customers a few days later. "And the place hadn't been rewired since the fifties, I reckon. Old Roger was bound to fall over in the dark one of these days; we're none of us getting any younger, are we? And those bookshelves were obviously unsafe. Nasty way to go, though – getting your head smashed in by a load of books."

Afturganga

Being one of the contractors who worked on Krafla had always given Simon an advantage in the geothermal sector. Few foreigners got the chance to be part of the Icelandic geothermal power plants, but everything had come together on that day back in 1975: a recently completed PhD on the energy potential of geothermal boreholes, an Icelandic doctoral supervisor with connections in the industry, and an unsated wanderlust in the young geologist. He took up the invitation without hesitation.

Everyone learnt a lot at Krafla; the early boreholes seemed successful, but by September it was clear the earth had no intention of co-operating. The tremors were subtle at first. Then, gradually, they became stronger and more frequent until drilling was impossible. Then, in December, bright orange magma began spewing from Leirhnjúkur, the mountain looming over the lava fields. There was nothing for it, and plans for the plant were abandoned. The angry earth stretched Krafla back and forth for years, and by the time construction resumed, Simon had a comfortable teaching position in England and little interest in getting back to the industry – and still less in returning to Iceland.

Now Simon was finally retired; and among the sycophantic embossed letters inviting the emeritus professor to consult on various geothermal projects around the world, he was surprised to find on his mat a handwritten airmail envelope with an Icelandic stamp. Handwritten post of any kind was a rarity these days, and Simon could not think of anyone he knew in Iceland who would correspond with him in that way – unless… But the professor of geology put aside that wild thought, which stirred in him memories he both cherished and feared.

He did not open the letter straight away. He was not sure he wanted to. The more Simon thought about it, the more he wondered whether this was, in fact, a letter from Heiðrún. After all these years, to his shame, he could no longer remember what her handwriting looked like; but it was a woman's hand, he thought. Finally, retreating to the bedroom, Simon tore open the letter, drawing out a thin piece of paper with what looked like a childish doodle of an envelope held up by ribbons with some sort of elaborate cross underneath it. Sure enough, on the other side of this odd doodle was Heiðrún's address, along with her telephone number and email address. A quick Google search of her address told him she was now in the south of the country, about two hours from the airport.

There was really only one answer to the question Simon had asked himself on opening the letter: "What possible reason could she have for writing to me now?"

Heiðrún was dying.

She might have months, or it might be weeks. She begged to see him; she even expressed remorse for leaving him all those years ago.

"I'll understand if you don't want to see me. But I don't want to go without seeing you once more. You'll understand that I can't travel; will you come to me, Simon?"

The pleading moved Simon, he could not deny it. And Heiðrún had done the right thing to write to him by hand; even that silly doodle reminded him of her obsession with old Icelandic designs, and the scarves she used to knit. Sitting at his computer, he began composing an email in reply. Within two days, after several more exchanges, Simon had bought a ticket to Iceland – not the first destination he thought he might visit in retirement, which came as something of a disappointment to Rose. Simon thought his wife had been dreaming of the Caribbean; he was hardly surprised when she declined to go with him to Iceland, and he was relieved too. Travelling with Rose would have required him to explain who Heiðrún was, besides being 'someone I worked with at Krafla' – which was not quite a lie.

*

Heiðrún's husband met Simon at Keflavík. Svali must have been at least ten years younger than Heiðrún; tall and muscular, with receding yet still red hair, and the intensely white skin and blue eyes of so many Icelanders. He seized Simon's hand in a firm grip as he introduced himself in perfect, barely accented English.

"Heiðrún's told me a lot about your days at Krafla!"

Svali was easy company on the two-hour drive to the farm where he and Heiðrún bred horses. Simon's fear that conversation would be awkward with a man married to a woman he once loved soon evaporated. For a husband whose wife was dying of cancer Svali was rather cheerful, and there was evidently little that Heiðrún had not told him about her relationship with Simon.

"Don't worry! Heiðrún and I, we've only been married fifteen years! It was a long time ago for you two, eh?"

"A different life, yes."

Svali swerved the four-by-four to avoid a large pothole in the narrow road. "I understand it, you know – her need to see the old faces."

"You're very considerate."

"I want to give her what she wants. You understand? I can't refuse her. Not now. I'm grateful you came all this way, believe me."

The farm was halfway up a grey-green ridge, where snow still lingered on the jagged summit; Simon saw the stocky, short-snouted Icelandic horses scattered in their paddocks before the old farmhouse came into view. It was a long, low, single-storied building, faced with bright red painted panels, with a corrugated iron roof.

"Turf originally, of course." said Svali, pointing at the roof with pride. "In my family for five generations."

"It's quite a survival," Simon remarked, knowing that few old houses endured Iceland's periodic outbursts of seismic rage.

"I love it!" Svali slammed the car's door and began striding towards his home, "And I love her. Heiðrún!"

He waved and shouted to his wife, who from this distance was a small, pale figure wrapped in a blue shawl by the farmhouse door. Simon had been dreading this part of the trip: seeing Heiðrún for the first time, and what the years and sickness had done to her. Just before leaving for the airport he had found some black and white photographs of his time in Iceland in a battered shoebox. Only one image of Heiðrún survived, standing against some street in Reykjavík in an oversized duffle coat, a slight smile on a face framed by that long, straight hair so popular in the '70s. The dirty snow piled behind her told him this was probably the spring of '76.

That long hair, now white, was tied tightly behind Heiðrún's head now. She looked at once older and younger than Simon expected; her thin arms shocked him, but the former Heiðrún was still there in that face, that wry smile. She made no movement towards him as he and Svali approached the house, but reached out to embrace him as soon as Simon was close enough to touch.

"You came!" was all she said.

*

It was difficult to forget that day, although Simon worked hard to do so. The rising heat beneath the two men warmed their legs as a stench of burning rubber mingled with the sulphurous smell rising up from the pale yellow volcanic tuff; it was like walking on the floor of a kiln, and the burning ground was melting the thick rubber soles of their boots. Here and there, steam poured from small fissures in the ground. It was early December, and at least ten degrees below – but there was no snow here, of course, nor on the bare peak of Leirhnjúkur. The distant hills were white, and merged periodically with a colourless sky – a perpetually vanishing and re-appearing horizon.

Their walk out onto the active lava field of Krafla was not official. The men's superiors might not have expressly forbidden such an expedition, but they would certainly have advised against it. The drilling operation was close to packing up; the tremors were becoming more frequent. Iceland was stirring again, and Simon wondered whether the drilling itself might even have made things worse – after all, they still knew so little about this extraordinary island, thrust up so recently from the bed of the North Atlantic.

Egill was striding ahead. In spite of the cold, he was sweating profusely and had taken off his knitted hat. Egill was one of those few dark Icelanders – descendants of Irishmen, Simon thought – and he wore his black hair down to his shoulders. Simon admired Egill's enthusiasm, but it did not erase his deep hatred for the man. Simon wanted Heiðrún to look at him like she looked at Egill. He could still hold a civil conversation with his fellow geologist, but his intense desire for Egill to be gone was primal – a churning magma chamber of jealousy that lay beneath the trappings of civility, professional courtesy and scientific discourse. He was never sure how much of this Egill knew; unless he was a complete idiot, the man had surely understood that Simon, too, was in love with Heiðrún. Perhaps he knew it, but blithely thought the polite Englishman would yield graciously when the time came for making choices. In any event, Simon planned to surprise him.

A few days earlier Egill had told Simon breathlessly that crustal separation was occurring – the Eurasian and North American tectonic plates that cut Iceland in two were actually moving apart, making new rifts in the Krafla lava field. Egill was itching to compare the new rifts with the last survey of Krafla, in an effort to calculate the speed of separation.

"The land's rising – it's the inflating magma chamber. It's going to be a big one, I think."

Simon no longer felt any guilt for what happened that day. Decades of analysing his own actions assured him he was blameless. He had no doubt that adrenaline took over from jealousy when he was frantically gripping Egill's hand over that rift. The risk of the fragile clay shelf crumbling beneath Simon as it had beneath Egill and the intense heat of the deep earth scalding his face and throat were all reason enough to let go – but he did not. He held on for what seemed like hours. Egill fell because the fumes rising up from that hell-hole overcame him, surely; his body went limp, he loosened his grip – and Simon could no longer hold on. There was no body, of course, but the *rannsóknarsvið* accepted Simon's story; after all, setting out on Leirhnjúkur in the middle of heightened seismic activity was unlikely to end well.

Nevertheless, Simon had felt guilty about it all for a long time. When you set out on a dangerous expedition harbouring murderous thoughts against your companion, and that companion loses his life in a tragic accident, the mind and the conscience play tricks. But if he was truly honest with himself, Simon was forced to admit he felt guiltier still about what happened afterwards – how he took advantage of Heiðrún's grief to initiate their relationship, even if those months with her in Reykjavík had seemed the happiest of his life. He never knew exactly why she left, although years later he guessed at it; the grief was wearing off, and as it did Heiðrún realised she had never really loved Simon. Without Heiðrún, Simon had no further reason to stay in Iceland; and when Iceland severed diplomatic relations with Britain he could not go back anyway. The escalating Cod Wars pleasantly absolved him of going back to tie up the loose ends, and by the time peace was restored he had a wife and a young child in Southampton. Iceland was over.

*

Heiðrún spent more time looking at Simon than talking to him that evening. She seemed subdued and distracted – the effect, Simon presumed, of whatever medications she was having to take. She asked him a few questions about Rose, and about his daughter and grandchildren. Svali was more voluble, as he had been in the car, pressing Simon on his knowledge of Icelandic geology and matching it with an equally vast knowledge of Icelandic folklore. Simon had always felt uneasy about this Icelandic tendency to populate every lava field, caldera, chasm and peak with ghosts, elves and trolls – a hopeless effort, he thought, to impose the human on the inhumanity of nature. Even the oldest stories were a mere blink in geological time.

Svali had been pouring out the *brennivín* freely and eventually retired to bed, leaving Simon alone with Heiðrún at last. She reached out her hand and touched his affectionately.

"Thank you, Simon."

He smiled nervously. "I had to come, of course. We never really wrapped things up, did we?"

She frowned. "We didn't. And I'm sorry. I was young; I suppose... I just didn't understand how much I was still grieving Egill."

Simon nodded. "I understood that too, eventually."

"That's good..." She looked up at the low wooden ceiling. "I don't think I've ever quite recovered from what happened. But you... you were there, Simon. At the end. I couldn't have borne it."

34

"Believe me, it's never left me either."

She looked straight at Simon now. "I've seen him, you know."

"Seen who?"

"Egill. His spirit. Whatever you want to call it. We call it *afturganga*."

Under other circumstances, Simon might have smiled indulgently. He could not do so now. Somehow, her assertion – however absurd on an objective level – had an unfamiliar solemnity to it.

"You don't believe…?"

She shook her head. "I didn't used to, really I didn't. But Svali knows how to do things. Ways we've forgotten."

"Ways we've grown out of, surely?" Simon gently challenged.

"Always the sceptic, Simon! Listen, pass me that book. Yes, up there."

At the top of the dresser, close to the ceiling, was a small book wrapped in some sort of ancient, blackened leather. Simon thought it might even have been sealskin.

"It's OK, open it. It belongs to Svali's family."

Simon peeled back the desiccated sealskin to reveal a few leaves of rough paper, little bigger than a passport, which were covered with crude diagrams and a few rudimentary Icelandic words.

"They're staves. Old Icelandic magic." Heiðrún explained. "Did you bring the letter I sent you?"

"Of course." Simon felt in his pocket and drew out Heiðrún's letter, which he had kept because it had her contact details. He was beginning to feel uneasy about this; he knew now that the peculiar pattern she had drawn on the paper was not just a doodle. He recognised it as a copy of one of the staves in Svali's book.

"It summons spirits," she said softly. "I wanted you to see him too. Now you will."

*

Simon wanted to tear up that paper into pieces and flush it down the nearest toilet. Out of respect for Heiðrún, he refrained. Simon did not believe in the supernatural – nor in God, come to that – but there was something peculiarly intrusive about someone trying to involve you in their own supernatural delusions. It was not fear of the supernatural that disturbed Simon, a man who had devoted his life to science; rather, this nonsense discomforted him for the same reason as Svali's tales of elves and trolls. The idea of an intelligent man like Svali thinking he could perform magic was faintly repellent, like a grown man playing with children's toys in the absence of any children. Relics like that so-called book had a place in a museum, he supposed – but to treasure them like this was deeply perverse.

The next morning, at breakfast, Simon found it hard to be civil with Svali. Was the horse-breeder deliberately feeding Heiðrún's delusions about seeing the dead Egill, like those despicable charlatan mediums? Or was he humouring his wife's desperation, and pretending to occult powers?

"You didn't see him, then?" Svali remarked, slurping another spoonful of *skyr*.

"Who?"

"Egill."

"You never knew Egill. Frankly, silly games like this are disrespectful to his memory." Simon sat down and began slicing some rye bread. "Where's Heiðrún?"

"Catching some extra sleep. For a man who lived in Iceland, you don't understand much about us, I think."

36

Simon was becoming angry now. "Is this the real reason you wanted me to come here? So you could show me a ghost?"

The mischievous smile dropped from Svali's lips. "It wasn't me. It was Heiðrún. It's brought comfort to her to see him. She thought it might help you too."

"With all respect to Heiðrún, she doesn't know what would help me. I get to decide what I believe in and what I don't."

Svali put up his hands. "Fair enough. If you don't see Egill, you don't see him. We can drop the *afturganga*. Coffee?" He motioned to the cafetière on the table.

"Svali, I'm grateful for your hospitality. But I think it's best if I leave today. I don't feel comfortable being part of whatever … of whatever story Heiðrún is telling herself. Maybe it does bring her comfort. But this sort of thing… it's not for me."

"You want me to drive you back to the airport?"

"I'll get a taxi, it's fine." Simon replied.

"Out here! You're crazy. Let me show you the farm, at least. Then I can drive you wherever you want to go."

Simon wanted badly to believe that something was salvageable from this disastrous trip. He felt as though Heiðrún's delusion about Egill had poisoned any chance he had of an honest discussion about the past. With luck, if he could get back to Reykjavík, he could have a couple of days exploring the city and seeing how it had changed before he headed back to London. But he saw no harm in seeing the farm; whatever else they might have been, Svali and Heiðrún had been hospitable.

The horses were undeniably lovely creatures – so unlike any other breed of horse he had ever seen. They were best compared to overgrown Shetland ponies, albeit in a greater variety of colours. Watching Svali brushing their long coats and manes was hypnotic.

"They're beautiful…" Simon reached out to touch one of the animals.

"It's good here. Wait till I show you the *laugin*!"

"You have your own thermal pool?"

"Thirty-eight degrees all year round. The fun we had in there as children, eh!"

Some of Simon's happiest memories of his time in Iceland were of the thermal baths; luxuriating in the water while he played chess or draughts on raised tables with old Reykjavikers while the frost gathered in his hair – or lying with his arm round Heiðrún while the two of them gazed at the stars in the clear heavens that arced above that strange, churning geological hell.

"You'll take a dip before you leave, won't you?" asked Svali. "At least let me show you."

The athletic horse breeder led Simon into what appeared to be a cleft in the hillside, which turned into a stepped descent towards a deep-set, roughly round pool. It was a cold day for March, even in Iceland, and steam mantled the pool's surface, but cleared as the two men reached the level of the water.

"It's odd, isn't it, that there's molten lava in the heart of the earth heating that water." Svali remarked.

"Not so odd if you've spent your whole career researching geothermal energy. But they're lovely things, and you have a special one here."

They were shielded on two sides by walls of black, mossy rock, while the open sides of the pool gave onto a slope too bleak even to pasture horses, and beyond that the distant peak and glaciers of Torfajökull.

"Some view, huh?" Svali gestured to the wild expanse.

On their return to the house Heiðrún was awake, but not well enough to leave her bed. Seeing her like this, her frail hands clasping a cup of coffee, Simon did not have the heart to say what he had to Svali.

"You'll stay another night with us, won't you?" she pleaded. He could hardly refuse; but the sense he had been brought to this place under false pretences warred within him with a desire to make the most of this chance to re-acquaint himself with rural Iceland – as well as the genuine sympathy he felt for Heiðrún.

"Of course I will, Heiði. But I must head back to Reykjavík tomorrow."

"I understand. I'm sorry if Svali and I... if we've offended you."

Simon sighed. "We all have to make peace with the past somehow. I do it in my own way. I'm not sure Egill has ever left me, really."

"Heiðrún needs to rest now, Simon." Svali was standing in the doorway. As he closed the bedroom door behind Simon he handed him a large towel.

"Now for that swim we were talking about."

"Well, I'm not sure I should..."

"Nonsense. It'll do you good. And no-one stays with us without trying the *laugin*."

It was certainly true, Simon reflected, that he might not get another chance to swim in a natural geothermal pool in Iceland – perhaps never again. He accepted the towel.

"Great! I'll leave you to it." Svali slapped him gently on the back. "Just don't slip on the path."

When Simon reached the laugin it was in deep shade, but the unobstructed view across the bare hills towards

Torfajökull was heart-rendingly beautiful. The flank of the mountain was transfigured by golden sunlight so that the glaciers shone with an almost blinding glow. Quickly, he took off his clothes and sat down on the hard rock, testing the bottom of the pool with his toes. The warmth of the water was perfect, like a newly drawn bath with a whiff of sulphur. As he lowered himself in his feet soon found the pool's sandy bed. Like all pools of this kind, the water temperature varied slightly in different places, and it was important not to go too close to the aperture where the pool opened onto its geothermal source. But finding a comfortable zone, Simon let himself float back in the water, gazing up at the cloudless blue sky and overhanging black crags. He began to remember how easy it was to drift into an altered state of consciousness in these *laugar*, which became watery cocoons separate from whatever weather was above and around them.

He must have allowed his eyes to close. A splash startled them open, and Simon pitched himself upright in the water. The air temperature must have dropped even further, as the mantle of steam almost obscured the mountain now. But Simon's eyes were drawn now to the surface of the pool itself. Something was moving in the warm water; no, not moving – emerging. Black, matted hair, then yellow shoulders of something like flesh, turning slowly to face him –

Simon lunged for the side of the laugin, gashing his knees on the rock, and scrambled out. Grabbing his clothes and towel in a single motion, and not looking back, he began to stumble down the slope beneath the pool.

Simon reached a road eventually; one with some traffic, luckily. He caught a lift from a woman driving towards Reykjavík to see her daughter. She must have been shocked to find a shivering man under a towel trying to hitch a ride on a remote rural route. Simon wanted to explain that it was not cold that made him shiver – but he struggled to say anything.

The Leaven of the Farisees

"I saw fairies dancing."

Victor knew, as soon as he saw them, that these were words he would never dare to speak, even though he believed them to be true. For he did see them; early one morning, on the other side of the lake, just as the mist was clearing. His face pressed to the cold glass of the sash window, he gazed at the group of figures – he never managed to count them – dressed in brilliant white, holding hands as they looped in a strange, melancholy, circular dance; it was as if they had been dancing forever, as if all they existed for was to make these steps and move together in this way. The sun, breaking through the leaves of the south wood, dappled their skirts as they continued their stately pace – too far away for Victor to make out any details, but close enough for him to be sure. Then his father was coming into the room, and he bolted from the window as if caught in the act of theft. He was eleven; and a thoughtful child, old enough to understand that he could never speak of this, neither to condescending adults nor to mocking peers. It wounded him to keep the secret; to keep it even as its impossibility deepened into a chasm in the cynical years of adolescence – but still he kept it to himself. He kept it, because however much he doubted, he still did not want it mocked. Anything else was fair game; but not this.

Thirty years later, Farrer's Hall was once again Victor's home. It had not been his choice; when his mother died, Victor wanted to sell the house, but Marina had clearly been looking forward to living here for years; and he could hardly deny his wife's argument that it would be wonderful for Wendy to grow up in Suffolk. The house was not large compared with many country houses in the county – smaller, indeed, than some of the gigantic former rectories their friends lived in. Victor's father had snapped it up for a tiny sum in the seventies when it was almost derelict. An enterprising Georgian architect had tried to make the medieval hall fashionable on the smallest possible budget, with a hastily erected plaster frontage and oversized sash windows stretched and pulled into uneasy rhomboids by shifts in the surrounding wattle and daub. From a distance, or with poor eyesight, the house looked elegant; close-up, it was a mess. But to Wendy it was magical, and that was what mattered; and the grounds were enormous.

That summer they had been in the house for just over a year. Victor thought he had ransacked the place from top to bottom – a job he had already spent many hours doing as a child – so he was surprised when a hitherto undiscovered cupboard came to light on the top floor, in one of the old servants' rooms. It was built into the wall, painted shut, with its little brass handle painted too, and the heavy wrought-iron bedframe pushed against it. Marina had been talking about painting the top floor, so he shifted the bed to examine the wall.

As he planned to paint the wall anyway, he had no qualms about satisfying his curiosity and prised the cupboard open. By the light on his phone he could see the wattles supporting the tiled roof sloping down inside the void, and a great deal of dust; and he was about to turn away disappointed when he spotted the curled grey corner of a book. A brief flicker of hope crossed his mind that this might be something interesting, or precious. It was just a Victorian Bible, as it turned out; but it was nevertheless a talking point with Marina, who loved the history of the house, and it was diverting to speculate on who, in the distant past, chose to shove a Bible into such an out-of-the-way place.

"A kid who didn't want to learn for Sunday school?" Marina laughingly suggested as she gently took the book. "Or a Christmas present someone really didn't want?"

"It's not much to look at. I'm sorry I couldn't find you a medieval manuscript!" Victor joked.

"No, it's wonderful. It's part of the story of the house, isn't it? I'll have to find a place for it where we don't lose it."

"Or Wendy doesn't draw on it."

They were standing in the kitchen, where Victor had a clear view of his daughter kicking up gravel in the yard behind the house. At least she was wearing shoes this time.

It suddenly occurred to Victor to look for inscriptions in the Bible. He knew people sometimes used to write family birthdays inside them. Disappointingly, there was no name on the flyleaf, and it turned out the book was just the New Testament, and not the whole Bible as he first thought. The only annotation he noticed, as he leafed through, was in Matthew's Gospel. In Chapter 16, someone had underlined almost an entire verse in black ink that the years had turned to burnished brown:

> How is it that ye do not understand that I spake it not to you concerning bread, that ye should beware of the leaven of the Pharisees and of the Sadducees?

The line stopped at the word 'Pharisees,' and in the margin next to the verse was a little doodle – what looked like a circle with a broken cross at the centre, filled with dots.

"Hey, look at this." he passed the open book back to Marina, who was sorting through the morning's bills at the kitchen table.

"Now *that's* weird!"

"What is it supposed to be … the doodle, I mean?"

Marina's eyes were bright with recognition. "I think I *do* know what that is, Vic. It's one of those fossil things – you know, like an urchin or something. Wendy found one just the other day in the old coach house."

She went to the door and called to the girl. "Wendy! Can you get that funny fossil you found the other day and show it to daddy?"

Her daughter grinned and ran past them towards the stairs.

"And take your shoes off before you go upstairs!"

Before long Wendy was back clutching what Victor agreed was some sort of fossil urchin; a steep dome covered with little nodules, divided at the top by what looked like a cross. It certainly did look a lot like what the Bible-scribbler was trying to draw.

"Where did you find it, Wendy?" Victor asked her.

"It was up on a beam! I was climbing…"

Victor cut her off. "I think it's better I don't know where you were climbing." Marina laughed. She was all for Wendy exploring; Victor, on the other hand, remembered some of the childhood accidents that befell him and his brothers and sisters in this place.

"I don't want it." Wendy said firmly.

"We'll reunite it with the Bible, then." Marina reached up to put both the book and the fossil on the shelf for recipe books by the Aga.

*

The July weather was as lovely as he always remembered it, although Victor looked ahead with dread to the long weeks of Wendy's school holidays. If last year was anything to go by, her schemes to entertain herself became progressively more dangerous as the summer went on. Luckily she had plenty of less adventurous friends whose parents were only too keen to deposit them for the afternoon at Farrer's Hall, and they generally preferred playing dolls in Wendy's bedroom to using the beams in the old coach house as a climbing frame. They were expecting one such visitor that afternoon, but Victor was up early to walk Cyrus. He did not often walk the dog, which was the way Marina usually liked to get her day going; and when he did, he rarely ventured to the other side of the lake. The grass over there, he told himself, was too boggy, and Cyrus would be caked with mud. But that morning the dog was more playful than usual and ran into the long grass of the south bank before Victor could call him back.

Victor did not like to admit, even to himself, the reason why he was reluctant to go into that lush space between the lake and the woods, but what he saw there made him eager to get the dog back to the other side. The grass grew even more verdantly in great dark-green circles on the little rise behind the lake. Victor knew a fungus caused the phenomenon, of course; but the perfection of the circles was unnerving. And now Cyrus seemed to be following them, bounding around and around the circles, then joining a new one to make a figure of eight. The animal's movement reminded him of something; and Victor realised he was rooted to the spot. He wanted the dog to come back to him, but his feet were tied by a mixture of fear, disgust, and unprocessed memory that congealed around him like a prison of amber. He knew he could not step on that grass; he could not, and he must not, because to name those things – to give them their common name – would be half way to acknowledging what he saw that morning as a child.

"I saw fairies dancing."

Then a wave of fear overwhelmed him, coursing through his body. He tried to smile; a grown man afraid of a memory, and a memory that was probably imagined, at that. But the terror was real enough, whatever its cause. Mustering all his strength, and abandoning the dog, Victor managed to move and started retracing his steps. As he turned towards the east wood he saw that the rising sun was shining through the leaves and dappling his shirt; and he thought he heard laughter, though whether inside or outside his head he could hardly be sure.

Fortunately, the dog followed him; and it was a good hour before Marina emerged downstairs, tousled from the shower, by which time Victor had regained some of his composure.

"Do you know, I think I might bake some bread today!" Marina exclaimed.

Victor winced. Her last attempt at bread rolls had not been a success. Still, it might keep Wendy occupied indoors.

He spotted Geoff, their part-time gardener, crossing the yard to the coach house – probably to get the ride-on mower. The man was a fount of knowledge on all things 'old timey' (in Marina's phrase), so Victor grabbed the peculiar fossil from the shelf and headed outside.

"Wendy found it in the coach house," he explained. "I thought you might know what it is?"

"Oh that! Tha'll be the farcy loaf."

"The what…?"

"Farcy in 'orses. When yon glands swell up an' that. 'Orsemen put 'em up in stables an' that; thought they kip off the farcy."

The old man was hauling open the coach house door, showing no further interest in the fossil. Pleased to have another nugget of information on the history of the house to share with Marina, Victor replaced the 'farcy loaf' on the shelf. While the name was a strange one, he could see why people might have seen the fossil as a little loaf.

*

The smell of freshly baked bread was filling the house; Victor was pleasantly surprised, his wife even more so.

"Goodness! It's the best loaf I've ever managed!"

It was, indeed, a lovely looking loaf; round, perfectly risen, and with a single cruciform split at the top. Not unlike the little 'farcy loaf,' in fact.

"Look, Marina – " he took the urchin down to show her. "You've made a big one!"

She laughed. "It does look a bit like that, doesn't it? Must be my lucky fossil! Get Wendy and we'll have some of this with lunch."

Wendy was so excited about the imminent arrival of her friend (whose name Victor could never remember) that her parents struggled to keep Wendy at table. They soon heard the crunch of a Range Rover on the gravel drive. After exchanging pleasantries with the parents and admitting the girl (who struck Victor as a blonder, taller version of Wendy), Victor intended to get back to work on writing his latest legal textbook. But the air in his study felt heavy. He could not concentrate; probably, he thought, it was too much of Marina's bread lying on his stomach.

In need of a walk, he put Cyrus on a lead and strolled down the drive to the main road; once over it, a footpath between a fallow field and some woodland led to the neighbouring village, whose church's spire peeked from behind some trees. Victor thought he might go up to the church and back. Cyrus was excited, his nose thrust permanently into the undergrowth at the fringe of the copse as he pulled Victor along at his own pace. The afternoon sun still stood directly above man and dog in a cloudless sky, denying them even the slightest shade. The dark cool of the untidy copse was beginning to look inviting. They were walking in an old plough furrow, and Victor had begun to regret not bringing his sunglasses when he stopped dead in his tracks. Cyrus was barking wildly.

A figure stood at the end of the field, directly in their path – smaller, Victor thought, than normal human size, and perfectly still; far enough to be obscure in the haze of afternoon heat, yet close enough for its reality to be undoubted. Cyrus was straining so hard at the leash now that Victor was doubled over trying to keep the animal under control; this, and the glare of the sun, made it impossible for Victor to carry out any close inspection. But he knew he was being watched; that much was obvious. He received an impression of mockery, even without discerning an expression. And, worst of all, and despite his own most rational inclinations, he felt this being was not human.

It was as hard to turn his back on the watcher as it was to continue walking towards it; but it was the only option available to him.

"Come, boy!" He pulled the snarling dog away, back towards the road.

Victor was relieved to run into Geoff mowing the lawn closest to the drive. The presence of another human being – any other human being – seemed to act as some sort of insurance against whatever eldritch horror was gradually impinging on Victor's waking life. The mower spluttered to a halt as Victor approached; Geoff had a question about replacing a part, but Victor paused him in mid flow.

"Absolutely, Geoff; anything you need. But can I just take you back to the house and show you something – just for a moment? Come and have a cup of tea."

"Well, I don't moind if I dew!" Geoff took off his cap and used it to wipe the sweat from his face. As they reached the back door, Victor gestured to the shelf above the oven and the 'farcy loaf.'

"Geoff, you remember I showed you that thing this morning? And you told me it was something to do with horses?"

"Thass roight; the farcy loaf."

He switched the kettle on and reached for two cups. "It wasn't the only funny thing we found. I also found that old Bible up there – yes, the grey one. In a painted-over cupboard at the top of the house."

Geoff brought it down, holding it gingerly like a man unused to handling books.

"The odd thing was that there's a picture in there – someone seems to have drawn your farcy loaf, and I just wondered if you had any idea what it meant. It's in Matthew somewhere…" Victor took the book from Geoff and began rifling through the pages. "Here!"

Geoff read the underlined verse aloud, very slowly and deliberately.

"Now there's a word 'ere – that word 'Pharisees' – when I think on when I wor a lad the old folks called fairies by that name. And some called that fossil thing a farcy loaf, and some a farisee loaf. My own grandmother told me her mother kip one hard by the bread oven – made the bread rise, she said."

Victor felt as though he was starting to make sense of some alien language; signs so strange that at first he had not recognised them as signs at all, but now began to disclose their secrets. He looked at the verse again.

"So … the leaven of the farisees – the leaven of the fairies – it's this fossil thing, isn't it? Because it makes bread rise? That's why there's a drawing of it next to the verse?"

Geoff scratched his head. "I s'pose yer've got some'ut there. I never cud make 'ead nor tail of 'arf o' these ol' woives tales. But I dew recall some fella sayin' they pulled 'em up in the fields wi' the plough; and they was little loaves baked by the fairies." The old man scoffed. "That make me laugh, that do; cos my ma said this 'ere 'ouse wor Fairey's Hall afore they changed it to Farrers Hall…"

Both men were interrupted when Wendy's blonde friend ran into the kitchen.

"I can't find Wendy!"

*

Victor and Marina often had only a vague idea of where Wendy was, but they had learnt to recognise patterns even in her love of freedom and adventure, and it was certainly unusual for Wendy to disappear in the middle of a visit from one of her friends. Victor's first thought was that the two girls had fallen out, and Wendy had gone somewhere to sulk. That was what Victor's head told him, anyway; his heart told him that something was very wrong indeed. Wendy finding 'the leaven of the farisees,' that accursed fossil, had suddenly flooded Victor's life with all this strangeness; he understood now that the little doodle in the Bible was a warning left long ago: "Beware of the leaven of the Pharisees …" How it was that he came to find that warning just days after Wendy found the 'farisee loaf' was a mystery to Victor. He was unsure whether he believed in God, but perhaps someone was looking out for him.

Victor knew, from his bitter experience of keeping the secret of the dancers, that for better or worse he was sensitive to this kind of weirdness. He hated the fact, but it was undeniable. And along with the secret, he had always carried with him one nagging worry that he never openly admitted even to himself. It was the worry that by the very act of keeping the secret, he incurred a debt; no performance is given for free, and they wanted something from him. No; they wanted something *of* him. And so far, he had refused to give it.

Marina was baffled by Victor's panicked resolution to find Wendy immediately.

"For Christ's sake, Vic – she's gone off hundreds of times. She could be anywhere. She'll be back in half an hour."

He was not listening. He knew his daughter would not be inside the house; and if she was hiding there, it hardly mattered. It dawned on Victor that there was only one place he did not want to find her. Gripping Cyrus's collar, and practically hauling the dozing beast from his basket, he shoed the dog towards the front door and opened it, scanning the south lawn as it sloped down to the lake.

It took him a moment to spot Wendy; she was wearing a green top that nearly blended into the grass, and she was almost at the lake. If he was honest about his own fitness, he knew she was too far away for him to reach her before she walked around the lake to the fairy rings. But someone might be faster than he was.

"Go to Wendy! Run, boy! Go, go!" He spoke to Cyrus in the same breathless whisper he used when exercising the dog in the morning. Mercifully, Cyrus entered immediately into the game, and set off at top speed across the grass. He loved to run into Wendy and see if he could knock her off her feet, and Victor was often astonished at Cyrus's speed. Victor started running too; he could not keep pace with the dog, but he wanted to get as close as he could. Wendy was turning to walk around the lake now; and against the dark of the woods, Victor could have sworn he saw figures now in the blue haze – figures dancing.

Then Cyrus caught up with Wendy. The dog ran in front of the girl and toppled her, giving Victor the crucial seconds he needed to reach them both, panting, bent double, and gripping his knees. Wendy seemed dazed, lying in the grass and blinking at her father and Cyrus. What she said chilled Victor as nothing else could.

"I just wanted to dance with them, daddy."

*

Victor took 'the leaven of the farisees' to the lake and threw it to the bottom. Then he returned the old Bible to its little cupboard; and he even dropped the rest of Marina's loaf into the compost bin. He knew they had not gone, of course; they were never gone. But getting rid of the 'loaf' felt like disposing of an invitation to them to enter his life. And when Marina's next batch of bread was scorched around the edges and failed to rise, Victor breathed a great sigh of relief.

The Ivetot Pedigree

The heraldic artist from London – Jim thought her name was Olivia, but wasn't sure, and was too proud to ask – arrived at two o'clock that afternoon bringing a large leather tube, at least three feet long. There was a special pleasure, he found, in receiving a luxury he knew he could not really afford. He stepped forward to meet the artist and take her hand as soon as she was in the entrance hall.

"Jim Ivetot. I'm so glad you could come in person. Rouge Croix recommended you personally, you know."

Her handshake was disappointingly limp, but Jim had come to expect that from young women these days.

"I was excited to see the house!" she exclaimed, although Jim did not think she looked especially excited.

"Yes! It's mostly eighteenth century – although the site has been in the family since the dissolution, of course."

"It must be wonderful to look after so much history."

Jim grimaced politely. It was an all-too-familiar platitude. How lucky he was to be the custodian of all this history and beauty! For custodian was all he was; the days when any Ivetot could add anything to the estate, or even alter a single stone, were long since past. There was no money, nor any leeway on a Grade 1 listed building. "I'm a glorified hereditary museum curator!" Jim sometimes joked when he had to say something to the visitors who crawled all over his house every Tuesday, Thursday and Saturday between March and October. It was not much of a joke; although Jim had long since accepted that Wolstanford was his life, whether he liked it or not, he was beginning to feel irked that his was a job where no retirement was possible, even at seventy-six.

"Yes." He replied, flatly. The woman was intelligent enough to realise she ought to cut to business at this point.

"Do you have a large table, perhaps, Sir James...?" She gestured with the tube she was holding.

"Just Jim, please – but yes, of course. Let's head into the dining room."

With a gentlemanly flourish, Jim held open the heavy mahogany door as they headed into a huge room scented with furniture polish, where the cold seemed to cling to the air and a vast, empty Georgian table sat resplendent on a threadbare Persian rug.

"Just here."

The woman carefully lowered the tube onto the polished surface and began to unfasten the lid, before reaching her fingers in to coax out the thick, expensive paper. Jim felt a thrill of anticipation – these days, an unfamiliar sensation. He knew it was an unnecessary indulgence; he knew he could not really justify it financially, but acquiring something new made a change from the constant worry generated by the grim spreadsheets he pretended to understand.

Then she opened it; lovely cream paper curled out to reveal a cobweb of exquisite blazons, each one glistening with blobs of silver and gold leaf. It was simultaneously familiar yet captivating, with formal yet flowing calligraphy in blue and red neatly clustered around each shield; the Ivetot spurs sparkled like stars in this exquisite heraldic art, which showed every significant marriage of the senior line of the family. There was Odo, Sieur d'Yvetot, the Norman knight who came over with the Conqueror (his arms, of course, were an anachronistic fiction); there were the six successive marriages of the extraordinarily uxorious Thomas Ivetot the Elder in the fifteenth century; and there was the prestigious yet unhappy alliance of the first baronet with the youngest daughter of the Earl of Hartismere. But vanity drew Jim's eyes, inevitably, to the bottom of the paper; to his own and Marjorie's arms, and to the differenced blazons of Jack, Melanie and Will.

The space the artist had left at the base of the pedigree, underneath the arms of his children, made Jim smile. For the first time, he felt genuine gratitude to this woman, rather than merely grudging admiration of her technical skill. He straightened himself up and stretched out his hand towards her.

"Olivia, I must tell you that this is absolutely splendid. Really, really quite beautiful."

The woman smiled nervously; he guessed her name was not Olivia at all, but she was too polite to contradict him.

"It's the space you've left for the grandchildren, if you must know. That was very thoughtful." His hand panned over the pedigree. She smiled more broadly.

"That's very kind of you. And I'm glad you like it."

"Did you know I'm about to become a grandfather? I can't remember whether I told Rouge Croix or not. And do for God's sake take a seat!" Jim gestured to one of the uncomfortable high-backed chairs along the edge of the room.

"No, I didn't actually – but I just thought, given your children's ages…"

Jim laughed. "You've got that right! They're certainly taking their time giving me any grandchildren. But Jack's wife is ready to pop any day now!"

"Congratulations." The woman offered quietly.

"Ha! Don't speak too soon, for God's sake!" He began pulling up another of the heavy chairs to sit next to her. "It's a family thing – we're always a bit careful talking about grandchildren. *Miseri Ivetoti nepotum destituti*, and all that."

The woman's interest was clearly piqued by the phrase. She sat up. "'The poor Ivetots, destitute of grandchildren'. Yes, I came across that phrase in the 1702 pedigree your assistant sent me. I was a bit puzzled by it – I mean, *nepos* can be translated as 'grandchild' or just 'descendant', so I wasn't sure what it meant…"

Jim chuckled. "It's a funny one. A family curse, if you can believe that."

"A curse?"

"Yes." Jim was quite delighted to find someone interested in one of his favourite stories about Wolstanford. "Come on, let me show you."

Standing up, Jim led the heraldic artist back through the Green Drawing Room and into the main hall.

"You must have noticed this?" He pointed.

Wolstanford Abbey was, on the outside at least, a local architect's poor imitation of the Palladian style – the consequence of a good deal of spending by an ancestor in the 1770s – but the building's interior was more of a mess. Although the fourth baronet had made strenuous efforts to remove any relics of the post-medieval mishmash beneath, some structural features had been harder to expunge. One of them was a huge pointed arch that divided the entrance hall from the library. The middle of the arch was filled in, but the stonework still stood proud of the dark red walls adorned with moth-eaten trophies of Victorian stag hunts.

"I saw it, yes." The woman nodded. "Part of the original priory, I assume?"

"It's the chancel arch, yes." Jim enjoyed talking about the priory – it was the part of Wolstanford's history that visitors rarely wanted to know about. "The Priory of Our Lady and St Wulfstan was a cell of Worcester. A pretty minor monastery, really. But there's a funny story about the dissolution. If you give me a moment I'll find the book."

Passing under the arch into the library, Jim opened one of the wire cages that protected the full Morocco bindings and pulled out a handsome copy of Spelman's *History and Fate of Sacrilege*.

"The visitors sometimes ask about it, so I keep the book near the door," he explained, and quickly found a marker in the page he was looking for.

"Here!"

He passed his visitor the open book, keeping his thumb pressed on the paragraph in question. She read:

At Wolstaneford, in Worcestershire, it is said that one Sir Roger Ivetot, who was at that very time in the course of breaking down the priory church of the black monks, was approached by a beggar seeking alms. Refusing the beggar, the unhappy Sir Roger was the recipient of this curse or, rather, admonition from the vagrant who, revealing himself to have been formerly a monk of that house, declared that neither Sir Roger nor any other Ivetot would ever live to see a grandson born to his house.

"And the remarkable thing is, I'm not sure any of us Ivetot men *have* lived to see our grandchildren," Jim interjected. "My grandfather copped it in the Great War when my father was just a boy; and when you look back through the family tree you'll see the same thing over and over again. I suppose you know it pretty well by now!"

The woman smiled nervously. "I must admit, I had noticed that none of the baronets lived into old age."

"I've beaten them all there, then! And I might just beat that old curse, too – touch wood!"

Just as he was reaching out instinctively to touch the bookcase, Lady Marjorie's head appeared around the library door.

"I trust my husband has offered you some tea!" Jim's wife exclaimed, as the baronet realised he had done little to satisfy the basic requirements of hospitality. The woman made her excuses; like so many people, she was clearly intimidated by Marjorie and did not relish the thought of taking tea with a pair of elderly aristocrats. Marjorie briefly viewed and politely cooed her appreciation of the pedigree before the heraldic artist finally left. Jim heard the door bang shut behind her, followed by the determined march of his wife's sensible shoes in the direction of the dining room.

"You stupid old fool. What do you think this is?" Marjorie gestured dismissively at the pedigree that still lay unfurled on the table.

"The visitors will love it when it's framed, darling…"

"The visitors! They couldn't care less who begat whom as long as they can prance around and pretend they're at Downton Abbey. This is for you, Jim, and you know it. And you damn well know we can't afford it, just when Jack and Catherine are going to need us. How much are you paying that woman?" She turned on her heel just as Jim was about to answer. "No, don't tell me. I'd rather not know."

*

Jim knew his wife's disapproval would pass – especially with the distraction of a new grandchild. Both of them were making sure they kept their mobiles on them at all times, but it was Jim who picked up a call on the landline that afternoon from his son Jack. Catherine was starting to feel contractions, Jack said, and they were heading into the John Radcliffe. Marjorie got terribly excited, but her daughter-in-law was at pains to insist that the birth might be a while off yet. "They'll probably send us home – better put the kettle on for a long night."

A long night it was. Jim sent Constance home at four, and Jim and Marjorie retreated upstairs to their private sitting room after a hasty dinner in the cavernous kitchen. Marjorie switched on the television for a short while, but it was not long before she declared her intention to go to bed.

"I shan't sleep, of course; I don't want to. But I'll try to read if I can."

"Very good, darling. I think I'll stick around for a while."

Jim was relieved at his wife's departure. He poured himself a tumbler of Scotch and, checking he still had his mobile in his pocket, headed back downstairs to the dining room. It was dusk by now; there should have been no-one in the immediate vicinity of the house, but the odd thing was that he distinctly heard someone shouting outside. A high, wheedling cry.

Perhaps it was a bird, he thought. Jim found the brass light panel in the dining room and illuminated the pedigree. He had been looking forward to examining it properly – but he was disappointed to see that he had been rather too hasty in praising the artist so highly earlier that afternoon. Jim could not be sure how he had made the mistake, but when he looked at the pedigree now there was barely any space at all below his children's names for the addition of grandchildren. Then he was interrupted again by that wheedling voice.

"An alms! An alms! For saint charity's sake, an alms!"

Both voice and words were quite distinct now; whoever it was sounded like they were right outside the window.

"Who the hell...?" Jim lurched for the window, but there was still plenty of light in the sky and he saw nothing. A few moments more and he stood at the top of the stone steps in front of the south door, a position that commanded the entire south front of the hall. There was no sign of anyone, and only evening birdsong.

"Bloody hearing things … that's all I need …" Checking his mobile as he re-fastened the locks on the door, Jim began to haul himself up the main stairs, feeling more than a little twinge of disappointment that the space he had imagined for grandchildren on the new pedigree had been a chimera after all. Jim settled onto the sofa in the sitting room. He was not sure whether he had dozed off or not when the vibration of a text message startled him out of his reverie. It was from his son.

"All good so far, seems like we're close. Midwife says baby by morning!"

Jim wondered for a moment whether he ought to show Marjorie the text, but concluded his son would surely have sent it to his mother too. He was beginning to allow himself to imagine what it might be like to be a grandfather – to hold the baby, to see the toddler running around Wolstanford, to play games in the gardens…

He certainly dozed off this time. It was completely dark outside when Jim awoke; more surprisingly, the light was off in the sitting room. He could only assume Marjorie had switched it off at some point – either that, or there was a power-cut. It was the latter, apparently, since nothing happened when he attempted to turn it back on again.

And there was someone on the landing.

"Marjorie!" He called out.

Someone was definitely moving out there, but Jim received no reply. His wife was not deaf in the slightest, so the possibility that a stranger was in the house sent a bolt of fear straight to Jim's stomach. Those stories of helpless old men and women clubbed to death in their own homes always frightened him; they reminded him of the injustice of growing old. There was a set of fire irons in the sitting room and he grabbed the poker before carefully opening the door onto the landing. There was enough moonlight to see quite clearly.

Sure enough, there did seem to be someone out there. On the stairs, in fact. Jim Ivetot doubted the evidence of his senses, but there was no mistaking that a cowled and hooded figure stood with its back to him, about halfway down. Jim was on the verge of speaking – of shouting, in fact, to demand what the stranger thought he was doing in the house – but the dryness of his throat, and an inexplicable sense that this moment was somehow *not normal*, strangled any sounds that might have come out. The baronet swallowed hard, and moved to the top of the stairs.

The figure was moving too, keeping a steady distance from Jim. At the base of the stairs it turned left towards the dining room. Compelled, Jim followed. He was now convinced that this was a vivid, lucid nightmare, and one he desperately wanted to be over. The cowled figure, still mercifully with its back to Jim, moved towards the table where the pedigree still lay, its corners curling slightly, while the gold and silver leaf caught glimmers of moonlight. As Jim grew closer, he realised something else had changed about the pedigree. Some words were scrawled beneath Jack and Catherine's names, and he recognised a horribly difficult Tudor hand similar to one he knew from his ancestors' estate accounts. But Jim already knew what those words were; he did not need to decode them.

Miseri Ivetoti nepotum destituti

Jim felt anger rising in him – towards his own subconscious, mainly, for inflicting a nightmare quite as horrible as this one, but also towards that monk – whom he knew was not real, but whose lingering presence mocked him as it had mocked his ancestors. Yet when Jim looked up the hooded thing was already on the move, sliding back towards the dining room door and the entrance hall. This time Jim did find his voice.

"Stop! Damn you, stop!"

The movement continued. Jim did not want to lose sight of the thing, but as he reached the dining room door he gasped. The monk was moving towards the library, but the wall that blocked the old chancel arch had vanished. The medieval stonework now framed a gaping darkness that seemed to stretch out arms of shadow to receive the monk.

Jim was beginning to contemplate the unacceptable. It was not a dream. The variety of sensations he was feeling in his body was simply too real; he was very much awake, and in any case, the fear that now convulsed him should have sprung him awake by now if he had been dreaming. His voice was feeble this time; he was pleading.

"What do you want, damn you? It was such a long time ago. I can't be punished for what they did. I can't … Please …"

Jim did not think he had taken a single step forward since he had reached the dining room door, but the floor seemed to be moving now – he could not be sure how, but the chancel arch was coming closer. The figure had vanished now, but just as arms of darkness had reached out to take the monk, so now filaments of black seemed to be curling out from whatever space of horror lay beyond the open arch. Jim did not need to move; the void beyond that arch had its own power. Whatever it was, it demanded to be sated.

"Oh God – I'm sorry!" Jim was sobbing. "God knows, I'm sorry for what they did! Can't I make it up? I'll sell the house, for God's sake – just let me …"

He tried to recall those imagined scenes of a few hours earlier – playing with a grandchild about to be born – but the advancing blackness was stripping away the future. Jim's mind was blank. He was passing under the arch now.

A few miles away in Oxford, and a few moments later, Jim's grandson drew his first breath.

The Devil's Breath

Lady Sarah cast her eyes over the words she had just inscribed in the accounts ledger, disbelieving that such an awful occurrence could be summed up in so few words:

> To the widows of the reapers killed in the
> fields by fire, £6.

Beyond the library's tall windows, dry heat shimmered above the desiccated south lawn of Silborough Hall. The library itself remained a cool sanctuary, with just enough light for writing. Lady Sarah Marden replaced her quill and sat back, watching the ink's black gleam sink into the pages of the ledger as she recalled the awful events of the last three days.

It had begun with a letter written by a man everyone in the world thought dead. Posted at Bristol, and written in the unmistakable crabbed hand of her brother-in-law, Saul Marden. Saul had been cashiered from the army at twenty-one, and declared his intention then and there to seek his fortune in South America. The inhabitants of that continent were then in open rebellion against the Spanish, and the riches of vast unexplored wastes lay open to the adventurous of all lands. So brother Saul, fulfilling all too well the parable, demanded of his brother the portion of his inheritance and took ship to Caracas. No more was heard of him until a report reached the British Consul in Lima that the body of an Englishman, strangely burnt, had been found by natives, high on a plateau in the Andes. A letter was discovered on the body, though unscorched by fire, from Sarah's late husband, Sir William Marden, to his brother Saul, and accordingly the Consul wrote to Sir William. The body had clearly been clad in English clothes, and was of a size and build unknown amongst the natives, the height roughly matching Saul Marden's. The evidence seemed conclusive: Saul had come to a sad yet mysterious end, perhaps killed by natives in a hare-brained search for the riches of the Great Inca.

But Sarah recognised her brother-in-law's hand immediately. There could be no doubt that Saul was alive. The letter, coldly inscribed in the third person, shortly informed Sir William's widow that Sir Saul Marden, now seventh baronet of Silborough, having taken ship to Bristol was now travelling post to London, from whence he intended to come in all speed to his seat at Silborough. That, once arrived, the baronet asked only to be left undisturbed in study and reflection, while he had every intention of making a handsome settlement upon Lady Sarah and her daughter, Sophie, whom he requested to remain at Silborough to continue the management of the estate. It seemed remarkable to Lady Sarah that a man as profligate as her brother-in-law should place the management of the estate before his own profit. The widow of an intestate husband, Sarah was conscious that she lived now upon Sir Saul's good will and pleasure, but she little expected the management of the estate to be committed entirely to her hands.

The extent to which Sir Saul intended to remain immured in study and reflection did not become clear until, three nights later, the thunder of hooves woke the household and a black coach careered through the park gates. It was well after midnight, and Lady Sarah was shocked at the state of the horses; they could not have been changed more than once between London and Silborough. The sweat poured from their flanks, and they were undoubtedly spent, but still the coachman could barely keep them from rearing up in terror, as if all the furies of hell pursued them. Lady Sarah, a shawl wrapped around her nightdress, moved to the door of the coach to welcome her brother-in-law, but was forestalled by a short man in a shabby dark coat with stock and preaching bands, who was the first to emerge from the vehicle. Rapidly explaining that his master was sick and in need of rest, he politely yet firmly asked Lady Sarah to step back from the coach as he hurried the muffled figure of Sir Saul up the steps of Silborough Hall and straight to the Chinese bedroom, on the first floor, which the new baronet had chosen as his sanctum. Lady Sarah followed, still hopeful of an interview, but the door closed behind the new master of Silborough and he was seen no more.

The next day, a heavy conveyance arrived from London bringing numerous travel-stained and battered cases. Sir Saul's chaplain, Mr Andrews (for this was the name of the unctuous and officious little man in preaching bands) carefully supervised the progress of these cases straight to the Chinese bedroom, but any expectation Lady

Sarah had of catching a glimpse of Sir Saul was disappointed.

"Sir Saul feels quite unable to take on the day-to-day running of the estate, Lady Marden," Mr Andrews informed her over luncheon. "He is sensible of your most excellent management of all the affairs of the Silborough estate since your husband's lamentable decease, and sees no reason why you should not, in the immediate term, continue in that most valuable office."

"You said that Sir Saul is ill, Mr Andrews – may I enquire as to the nature of his illness?"

The chaplain hid his hands beneath the table as if caught in the act of theft. "He is much enervated from the effects of the unwholesome climate of South America," was all the answer Sarah received.

The day after Sir Saul's arrival saw a remarkable change in the weather. What had been a fine English summer, with a brisk breeze and fine, scudding clouds in a blue sky changed in a few hours to a remarkably oppressive, windless heat. The sky was the colour of old damp plaster, a dull grey, but the sun's heat beat down with dry intensity. Lady Sarah began a short walk with her daughter along the lake that evening, but found the heat unbearable even after dinner. She found her eyes drawn to the black space of the window of the Chinese room, which resolutely refused to yield its secrets.

"How do you know that the man we saw last night really is Uncle Saul?" Sophie demanded. "I never saw his face. He could have been an imposter, like in *Udolpho*."

"You know I don't approve of you reading that sort of thing. Of course it's your uncle. I recognised his hand quite distinctly in the letter."

"But you never saw his face, did you? I think he's a banditto come to imprison us and murder us in our beds," Sophie Marden concluded with satisfaction.

"Really, Sophie! How can you say such frightful things?"

Sophie, however, was not listening to her mother's admonishment. She had stopped in her walk and was gazing towards the south side of the lake.

"Look, mama. How very odd. There isn't any wind at all."

Sarah followed her daughter's gaze and noticed that the sun had baked a patch of grassless earth on the south side of the lake, so that the soil had turned to the consistency of fine sand. A little swirl of the light brown soil was rising from the ground, coiling ever higher. Somehow, the total silence of the lake under that still-relentless evening sun, unbroken by the slightest murmur of wind or birdsong, filled Sarah was a sense that some danger was close at hand. She quickly took hold of her daughter's arm.

"Come, Sophie; I think we've walked long enough."

Her daughter looked at her for a moment, frowning in displeasure that her mother should cut short her curiosity, but made no resistance – causing Sarah to wonder if Sophie, too, sensed that all was not as it should be. Later that evening, as the darkness finally began to draw in, Sarah looked out from the library window and thought she saw a faint haze moving above the lake. Such illusions arose easily in the dusk, but she was glad nonetheless that her bedroom, and Sophie's, overlooked the avenue at the north front of the hall and not the lake to the south.

There was much, however, to distract Sarah's mind from such trifles, not least the matter of the harvest. Half a dozen fields were to be reaped the next day, and in accordance with tradition, Lady Sarah and her servants handed out beer to the village men in front of the hall. Gripping their scythes in one hand and their tankards in the other, the men grinned uneasily as they drank the health of the absent lord of Silborough – a lord most of them had not seen since boyhood. Already the heat of the day was intense, and the men were mopping their brows as if the day's work were done before they even reached the fields.

Around two in the afternoon, Sarah heard running feet on the gravel beyond the drawing room window, and saw two of the tenant farmers, Samuel Hunt and Nicholas Borley, tearing hatless down the avenue and towards the hall. Even from two hundred yards, she caught sight of a fear in their eyes that struck her to the heart. Instantly she remembered the strange light of apprehension that gleamed in the eyes of the servant whose task it had been to tell her of her husband's fall from his horse, six months ago – but this was more intense still. She found herself thinking of Sophie – but of course, the girl was safe; she had heard the notes of the harpsichord in the music room not five minutes ago. Sarah made her way to the entrance hall and forestalled the butler's protestations at the men's entering her presence wild-eyed and sweating.

"If it please yer ladyship, summat terble's 'appened up on Devil's 'ill," Samuel began, wringing his hands, and nearly bent over with anxiety. The hill stood on the land he tenanted, little more than a quarter of a mile southeast of the hall and easily visible from the grounds. Samuel seemed unable to continue, so Nicholas Borley took up the story.

"It ain't fit matter for a lady, ma'am – " he paused awkwardly, before deciding to continue; Sarah was, after all, the manager of the estate. "We cam' up that there 'ill not far arter noon, to see them boys waren't takin' too long over their bait, and Lor' bless me if they waren't all burnt to a cinder; them boys lyin' in the field, all black and horrible burnt up like, with only a little singein' of the corn around 'em."

Lady Sarah immediately called for Mr Andrews, the chaplain, and gave the governess, Miss Thurlow, strict instructions that Sophie was not to leave the house. She sent one of the footmen towards the village with orders to bring the constable, while she and Andrews set out towards Devil's Hill. Sam Hunt protested that it was no sight for a lady's eyes, but Sarah was determined to see for herself what the farmers had tried to describe. Mr Andrews puffed and sweated profusely under his wide-brimmed black hat, his eyes darting to and fro in anxiety, while Sarah pressed ahead confidently, lifting her skirts above the stalks of wheat that jutted from the baked earth. As they approached the summit of the hill she caught sight of a knot of men, eerily silent. They doffed their caps at her approach, faces stony with mingled grief and anger. As the men reluctantly parted, Sarah caught her first glimpse of the bodies. There were three of them, contorted and blackened, their scythes still gripped in claw-like hands, their faces turned upward in what could only be described as grimaces of horror – unless that was what the faces of men burnt to death always looked like, Sarah pondered. The skin was drawn back from their white teeth and eyes, where now there were empty sockets. As the farmers had said, the ground around the men was only lightly singed.

"My God!" Mr Andrews was holding a handkerchief to his face.

"Ne'er mind God. This wor the devil's work." A voice came from the knot of men, although Lady Sarah did not see who it was that had spoken.

"Cover these bodies'" she instructed, and a couple of the men took off their jerkins and placed them over the awful, grinning faces of the dead reapers. "Mr Hunt, Mr Borley," she called out for the farmers, who came forward sheepishly. "You are to remain here until the constable arrives, and take charge of the bodies." The men nodded, and with that Lady Sarah turned to leave. Mr Andrews began to chatter uncontrollably at her side.

"There are, of course, remarkable forces of nature of which even the profoundest natural philosophers have little knowledge, electrical marvels produced by disturbances of the atmosphere even on a cloudless day like this that might, perhaps, account for so tragic an occurrence; or perhaps a glass carelessly placed caused some fire among the dry wheat stalks that spread to the men's clothes, though why a common labourer should be in possession of such an instrument ...'

Lady Sarah cut him short. "Mr Andrews, I should like you to find out the names of the men that have died this day, and I shall draw two pounds for each of them, which I ask you to present to their widows as a token of Sir Saul's regret at this unaccountable accident."

Mr Andrews nervously nodded his assent. The constable came to see Sarah later that day, to tell her that there would be an inquest *post mortem* and that he expected the coroner to return a verdict of death by misadventure; the families had taken the bodies, but none of the men would go back to that field and finish the reaping. Sarah could not blame them. She also had a feeling that Mr Andrews had expressed more than just natural shock at the sight of the bodies; his reaction had been almost the shock of recognition – as if he had seen this before. He certainly knew more than his senseless babble suggested, and even his chatter suggested he was trying hard to find alternative explanations to avoid confronting a truth he knew all too well.

*

Satisfied the ink was dry, Sarah closed the accounts ledger and sat in silence in the library's cool shade. She thought she might try to extract the truth from Mr Andrews, but she suspected that strong bonds of loyalty to his master would make such an endeavour fruitless. She had no doubt that the events of that afternoon were related in some way to Sir Saul Marden's return to Silborough, and she knew that the only chance she had of finding the truth was to speak to Sir Saul himself. There was no use in hesitating, and she rose and made her way straight to the Chinese room, rapping smartly at the door. There was no answer.

"Sir Saul, I beg you to open this door. I understand that you have entrusted the care of the estate to me, but you cannot remain unaware of what terrible thing has passed this day. As your sister I implore you to let me speak with you."

To her considerable surprise, the door was opened without protest, and the tall figure of Saul Marden stood before her. He was, to an extent, as she remembered him; tall, olive-skinned, with an aquiline nose and lank, dark hair. She had always found distasteful the ironic sneer that permanently marked his features, and seemed to suggest contempt for all decency, and she was astonished to see that it had disappeared completely. In its place was a mask of fear, carefully concealed beneath a studied languor, but there nevertheless; and the baronet's olive complexion could not hide the cold pallor of a man awake for many nights.

"You must forgive me, my dearest sister." He stepped forward into the corridor, allowing Sarah only a glimpse of a room that seemed cluttered with books, instruments and what looked like feathers, before he closed the door of the Chinese room. "I have not been well. I fear that I am not the jovial lord of the manor I ought to be. Mr Andrews has made me aware of the lamentable events of this afternoon and I quite approve the alms you have distributed to the men's widows."

"Thank you, sir. Mr Andrews seemed ..." Sarah began, but was unsure how to continue.

"Yes?"

"I felt Mr Andrews might have seen something like it before."

The baronet's face darkened. "Did Mr Andrews tell you so?"

"No." She began to draw back from him, "I am sorry, Sir Saul, I am sure it was nothing but a woman's fancy. But the bodies of the men I saw this afternoon reminded me of the account the British Consul in Lima gave of the body we thought was yours – the one found in the Andes."

"And you think that a body in Peru could be linked to bodies burnt on a Suffolk farm?" A little of the old sneer was returning to his expression, but it only emboldened Sarah to continue.

"In both instances the connection was you, sir."

"You hold me responsible for the deaths of a thief who stole my papers, and three reapers on my land?"

"I did not say that I hold you responsible, sir ..."

Sir Saul reached out both hands and gripped Sarah's arms tightly, though not painfully.

"I refuse to accept that I am responsible for this," he raised his voice as he said it. "God save me from the devil's breath!" Anguished fear convulsed his face as he said it. "For God's sake, take your daughter and leave this place." He shook Sarah slightly, then abruptly let go of her arms, turned on his heels and went back into the Chinese room, slamming the door after him.

Sarah called Mr Andrews to the drawing room immediately, and instructed him in the plainest terms to explain how he came into Sir Saul Marden's service, and to tell her what he knew of those strange words, "the devil's breath." The clergyman sank heavily into a chair, mopping the sweat from his brow with the same handkerchief he had used to hide his face on Devil's Hill.

"I cannot tell you, madam."

"You *will* tell me, Mr Andrews. Sir Saul has already told me enough for me to know that he was somehow the cause of the deaths of these men – the mysterious traveller in the Andes and the reapers that died today. If you are a man of God, I charge you that you make this thing known to me if my life and the life of all in this house depend upon it. Are we in danger?"

"We are all in danger, madam ..."

"Then tell me the whole truth: it is your duty as a Christian."

Reluctantly, and perhaps deciding that she already knew too much of the affair, Mr Andrews told his tale.

Andrews was the son of a poor family, but was fortunate to enjoy the patronage of a gentleman, and so was enabled to study at Cambridge and take holy orders; but with the gentleman's death there was an end to his patronage, and he was forced to leave these shores to seek employment as a missionary. He first encountered Saul Marden in Lima, a man broken by fear who told him a wild tale, in which he and his companion, a Mr Lewis, had happened upon the tomb of some heathen king and despoiled it of great treasures of gold. Thereafter Saul declared that a shapeless and abominable thing pursued them, not to be named. It rose up from the sands in a cloud, or bubbled up from rivers in a steam, or fell from the heavens as blue fire to bring madness and death. They soon cast away the treasures into some chasm, but to no avail; the thing would not kill them, he said, but would pursue them and drive them mad until they should freely offer themselves to it; this, he said, had been the fate of Lewis, who one day could bear their terrible flight no longer and surrendered himself to the dark power upon a mountaintop.

With Lewis dead, Saul Marden decided that he, too, was better dead than alive; so he placed the letter from his brother about Lewis's person, trusting that Lewis's body would be discovered and identified as his own. Thinking that by changing his identity he might thereby escape the curse, and outrun this power as Jonah thought to outrun God, Saul journeyed to Lima, taking the alias of Paul Silborough. He was overjoyed to meet Andrews, a fellow Englishman. At long last, however, Saul could not forebear from confiding in Mr Andrews his terrible secret; at which the two swore, upon the Holy Bible, that they should find some way to lay this spirit. Mr Andrews sought counsel of the Roman Catholic priests in that country, but they dismissed the curse as idle superstition. Saul, however, heard from the natives of a horror in the high mountains they named *el aliento del diablo*, 'the devil's breath,' that tormented and burnt men who dared to defile the tombs of the dead.

Before the two could learn more, news reached them of Sir William Marden's death. Saul, who had not seen any sign of the thing since his arrival in Lima, sensed that liberation was at hand, and began to dismiss his earlier experiences as the delusions of a mind wearied by hard travelling. He determined to go back to England. The men took horses and set out with a party to Colombia, but as they did so a sandstorm rose up, and hid all the riders apart from Saul and Mr Andrews; and this was no natural sandstorm, for as they spurred their horses on they heard the screams of men behind them inside the whirlwind, and when the sandstorm lifted the road was empty. With no course but flight, they abandoned their ride to the Atlantic and took ship from Guayaquil around Cape Horn, Saul Marden ordering the rest of his possessions to be sent after him.

"But I see clearly now," said Mr Andrews, sobbing, "that there is to be no escape from this curse, not even in England. There is no hope for us."

Under any other circumstances, Sarah was sure she would have dismissed Mr Andrews's story as the ravings of a madman; but the expression she had seen on his face that afternoon, together with her alarming encounter with Sir Saul, convinced her that the force Sir Saul had awakened in South America lay outside the boundaries of reason. Nevertheless, she was reluctant to heed Sir Saul's advice and leave Silborough Hall immediately; after all, the management of the estate was committed to her hands, and the events of the day had proved that the ordinary folk looked to her for leadership. She could not betray their trust by leaving. And yet she wondered what other destruction might come to these poor people if Sir Saul and Mr Andrews failed to find some way to lay this awful power. That night, Sarah insisted that a bed should be made up for Sophie in her own room, and although her daughter was reluctant to be treated so much like a baby, she had clearly been shaken by rumours of the day's events, gathered from the chatter of the servants and her governess, Miss Thurlow.

"Miss Thurlow said that you have seen Sir Saul – what did he say to you, mama?" Sophie demanded as the lady's maid combed through her hair before bed.

"Only that he regretted his indisposition did not allow him to be more sociable."

"But didn't you tell him about the awful thing in the fields – what did he say?"

"Of course he very much regretted the deaths of the poor men."

"He sounds a very dull gentleman indeed," Sophie declared as she climbed into bed. "But I heard the servants saying he brought a curse with him to England and the horrible burning was for him."

Sarah sat up in bed. "How dare you bring me the servants' idle tittle tattle – " she shouted. Her daughter fell silent. Then, after a few minutes, Sophie said softly, "So it is true, then."

Sarah saw already that her overreaction to her daughter's words betrayed the truth. "He labours under a very heavy burden," she confessed, "but I believe he is a good man, for all that. Try to sleep, my dear."

There were two candles burning in the room, one by Sarah's bed and one on a commode beside the truckle bed that the servants had brought in for Sophie.

"Must I put out the candle, mama?" Her daughter asked. Sarah promised that she would stay awake. But as she moved to blow out the candle, Sophie screamed. The flame next to her bed was burning blue, and steadily lengthening; Sarah could scarcely believe her eyes, but not only did the flame lengthen – it also seemed to broaden out, into something that she could fancy was beginning to resemble a face with a mouth and eyes. Sophie had darted out of bed towards her mother, but as she approached Sarah's bed, her mother's candle began to turn blue as well. Gripping Sophie tightly and pulling her close to her, Sarah grabbed hold of a shawl and the two left the bedroom together. Sophie's scream had already roused Miss Thurlow, who stood with a candle of her own on the landing. As soon as she saw another candle, however, Sophie broke free from her mother's grasp and ran towards the stairs. There was a bright full moon, and its light was sufficient to see by in the stairwell and the white marble vestibule. Sarah called after her daughter, and at that moment the door of the Chinese room burst open and the figure of Sir Saul Marden appeared silhouetted for an instant against the light.

"Good God, woman; for God's sake don't let her leave this house!"

In a moment, Lady Sarah and Sir Saul were both running after Sophie; the great door of the vestibule stood open, and Sarah caught a glimpse of her daughter's white nightgown disappearing down the avenue. The girl must be mad with terror, she thought, or she would never leave the security of the house. As they reached the steps of the hall, however, a blurred darkness seemed to form between them and the figure of the girl. Sarah slowed down, bemused by what she saw.

"Go back!" Sir Saul called. "It's too dangerous for you." He pushed his sister-in-law towards the hall with main force. She briefly felt a thick, comforting darkness closing around her, but as Sir Saul ran further along the avenue it dissipated, leaving a cold chill of terror instead. Sarah retreated to the steps of the hall and wrapped her shawl around her, a powerless witness to what happened next. A faint blue mist, shot with glowing sparks, was forming above the running form of Sophie. The girl must have felt something, for she stopped, and looked up, as if transfixed by the stare of a wild and dangerous animal. The thing above her grew and pulsated, a sphere of glowing blue light almost as bright as the moon itself, and a blue halo appeared around Sophie's own head.

The tall figure of Sir Saul Marden had stopped just a few feet in front of her. Slowly he raised his arms towards the thing, and Sarah caught a few words of a strange, barbarous language: but these were drowned out as the sphere dissolved into a single bolt of blue fire that struck at the heart of Sir Saul. As it entered into his body, the fire disappeared as if it had never been, and he fell heavily to the ground, stiff as if turned to stone. The change in the air that came at that moment was palpable: the strange, dry warmth lifted, and the English night was restored, with a girl standing shivering in her nightdress under a bright moon.

Sarah ran to her daughter and enfolded her in her arms. The blackened body that lay at her feet was hardly visible, but Sarah knew that Sir Saul Marden had finally stopped running, and accepted his fate.

The Dreamt Book

Jocelyn was relieved to escape the full force of the downpour; the few people taking refuge inside the bookshop looked very bedraggled and sorry for themselves. She had no umbrella for the walk back to Euston Square, but hoped the worst might be over by the time the bookshop closed. Few people went out as well prepared as the man just coming into the shop now, with a knee-length overcoat, brimmed hat dripping like an overflowing gutter, black leather gloves and an expensive-looking umbrella. He dropped the latter in a container by the door before striding towards the very same shelf Jocelyn herself was browsing – not that a word like 'browsing' was quite adequate to describe Jocelyn's desperation to find a book that might help her.

The Dream was back.

The Dream (she mentally capitalised it to distinguish it from any others) often varied in its details, but always ended in the same way. She knew, of course, that this was common for recurring dreams. But most recurring dreams were nightmares, and this dream was hardly a nightmare;

not, that is, in the conventional way. It was not accompanied by, and did not generate, feelings of terror. But The Dream had turned Jocelyn's life into a nightmare; of that there could be no doubt.

*

It began when she was nine years old. One night she dreamt she was walking over a narrow, hump-backed bridge towards a raised bank of earth, held in place by the gnarled roots of trees, and carpeted with bright green grass sprinkled with beautiful flowers. As she came closer, Jocelyn caught sight of a slight gleam from a dark hole under one of the trees, and saw that it was the sun glinting on gold tooling that was part of the rich binding of a book, lying there half-buried. She reached down and drew out the book; it was large and very heavy, bound in sky-blue leather decorated with strange characters in black and gold, including a gold sun and silver moon. Balancing it carefully across her outstretched arms, Jocelyn opened it.

By means of the omniscience that so often accompanies dreams, Jocelyn knew this was a book of tremendous enchantment and power. But at the very moment when she was about to open the book, the dream always ended, or Jocelyn woke up. Sometimes she thought she caught a glimpse of pages filled with dazzling secrets, but she could never recall anything beyond the haziest of impressions. Yet whenever Jocelyn awoke from The Dream, she felt as though she had been on the threshold of discovering all secrets – even the meaning of reality itself. This feeling was not distressing; on the contrary, it seemed to imbue everything with a residue of magic for a while afterwards. The world seemed a little less humdrum after The Dream.

The Dream began to turn into a nightmare that same afternoon, in Mrs Sayer's lesson at the end of the day. In her sing-song Welsh accent, the teacher asked the children to write about a dream; what they dreamt about last night, perhaps, or any dream they remembered. Jocelyn sat for a long time, chewing the end of her pencil. It was a hot day, almost the end of term; all she could focus on was the sound of an aeroplane high above the empty playing fields, and the irksome smell of graphite in her nostrils; she thought of The Dream, of course, but somehow it seemed too private to share just yet. She quickly made up a dream about princesses and ponies, the sort of thing a girl of her age was supposed to dream about. But she had no plans to offer to read hers to the class.

In the event, Mrs Sayer had no volunteers; and she picked on a nervous boy named Lloyd, who was new to the class that term. Hesitantly, Lloyd began to read his dream.

"Last night I dreamt I was on a little bridge. Then I found a book under a tree. It was hidden in the roots. I picked up the book. It was blue. There was a sun and moon on the book, and black letters I couldn't read. I opened the book."

Mrs Sayer commented that Lloyd's account was a little short, and advised him to use his imagination to expand the story. She did not notice that two of her students had gone white; not only Jocelyn but also Ryan, the natural leader of the boys in the class, who glanced over at Jocelyn when he saw the expression on her face too.

In the playground, at the end of school, Ryan sauntered over to Jocelyn – carefully, she thought, so that no-one noticed him speaking to her.

"That was a funny dream, wasn't it? The one Lloyd had. About the book."

"Yeah…" Jocelyn eyed him warily. She wondered which of them would admit first that they, too, had seen the book last night. Ryan looked around him awkwardly. Jocelyn realised she would have to say it.

"It was my dream. He read my dream."

looked at her. "*Your* dream? That was what I dreamt last night. All of it. Every bit."

"So we all … had the same dream?"

They did not tell Lloyd straight away. Ryan said he was still not sure if Lloyd had heard about The Dream from someone else, even though Jocelyn insisted she had told no-one, and Ryan swore the same. Eventually, after a few days, Jocelyn and Ryan trusted one another enough to accept that each was telling the truth, and then they cornered Lloyd. He was terrified, but when they pressed him, they found he could describe The Dream in every detail.

A few weeks later, all three children had The Dream again. None of them was eager to admit it; but they each saw it in the others' eyes, and eventually Ryan was the first to say it. And so it continued, with no fixed pattern that any of them could guess; sometimes weeks passed, sometimes days, but always The Dream came back. They knew they could not tell parents, siblings, or teachers; and as the new school year passed, The Dream forged them into a tight-knit group of friends. They often discussed what it might mean; what the mysterious book might be about; and whether the bridge and the earth bank where each of them always found the book was a real place. Lloyd wondered why, if they always had The Dream at the same time, they never saw one another.

"Maybe because it's not us doing it. Maybe it's someone else's memory," Jocelyn suggested, "Maybe someone's sending us a dream about where to find the book because … well, because that someone can't."

"Like a … a dead person?" Ryan stuttered.

Jocelyn shook her head. "I don't know. But I'm not sure I'm me in The Dream, even though it feels like I'm me."

All three of them set alarms early in the morning, to make sure they woke up midway through The Dream, in the hope of recalling it better. Lloyd kept a pen and paper by his bed, and one morning he managed to draw some of the symbols on the front of the book, but the other two were not entirely convinced by the results. Nevertheless, the drawings went into a file the children were building on The Dream, and which Ryan kept at home and brought into school in his satchel.

Then came the end of primary school; Ryan and Jocelyn ended up at the same secondary school, but Lloyd went somewhere else. Their parents were not friends, they did not see each other in the holidays, and Lloyd had never bothered to tell Ryan and Jocelyn where he was going – so Lloyd disappeared from sight (so Jocelyn believed) forever. And Ryan seemed different now; anxious to maintain his position as top dog among the boys at secondary school, he adopted a callous, contemptuous and sarcastic persona. Boys did not speak to girls here; and when Jocelyn did once corner him and ask to see the file on The Dream, she was horrified when he told her, laughing, that he had thrown it away.

"You're such a stupid baby, Joss. Go ahead, keep looking for your magic book."

Jocelyn cried angry tears. She knew Ryan was still dreaming when she dreamed; but his reputation among the boys mattered more to him than understanding The Dream. Jocelyn was still more heartbroken when The Dream stopped, not long after her twelfth birthday. It became a childhood memory; one of those strange, half-remembered weirdnesses of growing up, which the teenage mind could no longer process – an object of ridicule rather than wonder. By the time Jocelyn was sitting her GCSEs she scarcely ever thought about The Dream; but she thought a great deal about Ryan, who had certainly achieved his dream of dominating the year group with his charisma. He was the boyfriend every girl wanted – or thought they wanted – and most of the girls whom Jocelyn thought a good deal prettier than her had their chance at one time or another; and by all accounts Ryan treated them terribly. Jocelyn remained fascinated nonetheless. But to someone like her, of course, Ryan was a distant fantasy.

In the final year of Sixth Form, when Jocelyn was preparing for her A Levels, everything suddenly changed. Jocelyn was often one of the last students to leave the Sixth Form workroom at the end of the day, where her peers jostled with one another to use a few pathetically antiquated computer terminals. Jocelyn had even managed to become room monitor, with the job of checking the computers were turned off at the end of the day. That afternoon, she was surprised to finish her duty only to find Ryan standing awkwardly by the door, clutching his jacket and bag, and staring at her with an alarmingly serious expression. He spoke with difficulty.

"Joss. I don't know whether you remember ... I barely remembered myself; but I had The Dream again."

Jocelyn's first thought was delight that Ryan was speaking to her; she would have been equally delighted if he had done nothing more than ask her the time. Her second thought was to wonder why, if Ryan had dreamt The Dream, she had not; as far as she knew, the two of them had never dreamt it at different times before. Her third was to wonder how she should respond to this extraordinary opportunity to capture Ryan's attention. What became clear, over the course of their conversation that afternoon, was that Ryan was not really as callous and acerbic as he pretended to be for the benefit of his legendary status. Alone with her, he was humane, vulnerable and warm. If Jocelyn had not been in love with Ryan before now, by the end of that conversation she was.

Just as she had hoped, that night they both dreamt it. The old feeling of magic returned, heightened a thousand times for Jocelyn by feelings she thought were love. And just as she hoped, Ryan wanted to carry on talking about The Dream, and to understand it. They carried on dreaming together, and the two of them began to search the internet – as painfully slow as that was in those days – in the hope of finding something out about the book, but to no avail.

"When we were kids we sort of assumed it was real," Ryan reflected one day, "but dreams aren't real. Not in that way, anyway. They're symbolic. So we need to find out what the symbols mean."

"But you threw away the file we made, didn't you? That had Lloyd's copies of the letters in it."
Ryan grinned sheepishly. "Joss, I didn't really throw it away."

She punched his arm theatrically. "You bastard! You just pretended? Just to impress everyone?"

"It was stupid. But yeah, I've still got it. In my mum's garage somewhere."

Sure enough, Ryan produced the file a few days later; and he and Jocelyn began adding to it. Jocelyn knew that she was only bringing new ideas to Ryan so she could have an excuse to spend time with him; and she began to notice him paying more attention to her, even when they were not talking about The Dream. The transient girlfriends vanished from the scene. She began to allow herself to hope; and then, on the hot summer afternoon of sports day, it happened. A few hours elongated into a single luminous hallucination of eternity; Ryan became hers. She was Ryan's girlfriend and, by extension, the girl everyone else wanted to be. Exams ended and school petered out into a seemingly endless summer of ecstatic discovery, and their dreaming together seemed to intensify Ryan and Jocelyn's relationship. They came to think of themselves as special, different – not like the fair-weather couples they saw fall in and out with one another among their friends.

But the endless summer ended. Pledging to visit one another as often as they could, they both headed to university in different cities. Long, passionate emails flew between them day by day, hour by hour. They ran up huge phone bills late into the night, and even managed a few visits. But the train was expensive; the phone calls gradually became shorter, and the emails less frequent and less effusive. Jocelyn knew the truth before Ryan had the courage to tell her. For Jocelyn, in a single moment the spell of love was broken; and she wished The Dream would stop, since she knew it still united her to a man she now hated. Knowing it would come, she tried not to sleep; and when she finally dozed off and The Dream overtook her anyway, the enchantment that always accompanied it arrived as vile mockery.

Drinking came first, then pills. Eventually, she found a combination that guaranteed her a dreamless sleep. Sometimes she took too many; one night she woke up in hospital, then found herself in a psychiatrist's office. University was suddenly over; she was back in her parents' house, back among her childhood toys, trying to understand why her life felt like a dream, and why The Dream now seemed more real than what people called reality. Her whole life was now reduced to a dream she had no hope of understanding.

*

The man in the felt hat smelled of expensive cologne; the tips of his white fingers skipped lightly over the books as he finally decided to pull out a dictionary of dream interpretation.

Jocelyn was not sure why she said it. You just didn't speak to people in London.

"I've got that one. Don't bother."

He looked up with a kind smile, framed by a red beard and meticulously manicured moustache. "Thanks. You've saved me the bother."

Something about the man's face was faintly familiar, but Lloyd recognised Jocelyn before she had the chance to see beyond the designer beard to the chubby and diffident nine year-old she once knew.

"You don't recognise me," he slid the book back, "But I remember you. You're Jocelyn Belsey. We were at primary school together. I'm Lloyd Prentiss."

Jocelyn lifted her hand to her mouth; she now understood the cliché, as she really could not speak; too many feelings warred within her to make it safe for her to utter any sound in a public place. She covered her mouth because she was not sure what expression her face would end up making. Lloyd was nodding affirmingly.

"It's OK. I'm sorry I gave you such a shock. What are the chances, eh?"

What were the chances? Jocelyn knew, and she thought Lloyd knew, that chance had nothing to do with it. Two people who last spoke about a shared dream when they were twelve, meeting decades later in the dreams section of Treadwells – that was the very definition of a non-coincidence. She was still silent. Lloyd continued, undaunted.

"I'm guessing you're here for the same reason I am?"

Jocelyn slowly lowered the hand from her mouth.

"Lloyd. Oh my God. Wow. Yes ... I came here, I heard they had books about weird stuff. I just thought ..."

"You had The Dream last night too, then?"

He was refreshingly direct. She respected that. Jocelyn nodded solemnly.

"Listen. This is incredible. Do you live in London?"

"No ... I got the train from Stevenage – "

"Even more amazing. This could be the breakthrough, Jocelyn. I know we hardly know each other, but do you think we could help each other out? I mean – we're kind of in this together ... ?"

Until now, The Dream had been inextricably entwined in Jocelyn's mind with the debacle of her relationship with Ryan – water under the bridge, in and of itself, if it had not been for the addictive tendencies that crashing out of that relationship unlocked within her. She had no hesitation in blaming Ryan for ruining her life. Maybe the relationship would have run its course; but for him to end it then, when they were still dreaming together – that was something she could not forgive.

Jocelyn and Lloyd stepped out of the bookshop into Store Street. It was still drizzling. He immediately unfurled his umbrella and held it chivalrously over her.

"So you decided not to buy anything?"

"I just don't know what would help. Those books have got a lot of stuff about the meaning of dreams. They don't say anything about people having the same dream at the same time."

Lloyd nodded. "True. I've really struggled to get any further over the years."

"You've struggled … ? But that means you have got further?"

"A little, yes. It sounds like we've got a lot of catching up to do. Where are you going? I'll walk you there."

"Only King's Cross."

"We don't have long, then! Or can I tempt you to stay? We could grab something to eat."

Jocelyn could not usually afford to eat in London. She could tell instantly, from the way he dressed (and even the way he smelled) that Lloyd had money. And that chivalrous gesture with the umbrella told her he was the sort of man who would offer to pay the bill for her. A few years ago Jocelyn would never have thought of taking advantage of insights like this, but she was past caring about social niceties like that now. Of course she would take him up on his offer of dinner.

"Great! I'll grab us a cab." He had thrust his hand into the air and hailed a taxi before Jocelyn had a chance to catch her breath.

Lloyd was curious about Jocelyn's life after they both went their separate ways. There was a lot to tell; and she was fairly honest in her account, even confessing to the pills and booze. She told Lloyd about her relationship with Ryan, about how her subsequent boyfriend abandoned her with a daughter, about her worthless ex-husband, about her divorce, and about her dead-end job. The only thing she omitted to mention was how it was fear of dreaming The Dream again, as well as the break-up with Ryan, that originally drove her into addiction.

"Wow. That's … quite a life story. I don't think I can compete with that. Thank you for being so frank."

"You seem to be doing all right for yourself. Better than me, anyhow."

"It's a gig in the City. Tedious, believe me. But yes, I'm paid pretty well."

"Any family?" Jocelyn felt entitled to probe after laying bare her own troubles.

"It's just me and Laurence. And I have a project that keeps me busy, after all."

"You mean trying to understand The Dream?"

"I mean the book. The Dreamt Book."

Jocelyn scoffed. "What? You really think it's an actual book?"

The cab was nudging its way through crowds in Soho now. "Just here!" Lloyd called out before he had a chance to answer Jocelyn's question. "I think you'll like this place," he remarked, as he led her down a side street to a small pub that served Greek food. Jocelyn was not picky; free dinner was free dinner.

As they settled into a paneled recess not far from the bar she reminded Lloyd he needed to clarify what he meant about the book being his project.

"Do you remember I once tried to remember some of those letters on the front of the book and write them down?"

Jocelyn nodded. "Yes. Ryan kept it in the file we made. God knows where it is now."

"Well, I tried it again a few times. I got better at it; the letters were clearer every time, and I was more and more certain I'd got them right. Eventually, I decided to show it to someone – a librarian at the Bodleian in Oxford. This was ten years ago. She's incredible – knows pretty much every alphabet there is. Well, she didn't know what it was but she said it looked familiar; so she showed it to someone else, a Classicist, and he identified it."

Jocelyn leant forward. "So ... ?"

"You won't believe this, but the Professor thought it was some ancient Spanish alphabet. Tartessian, it's called."

"So what does it say?"

"That's the thing; he didn't know. It starts with an 'I'. There are lots of Tartessian letters we can't read, apparently."

"Well that was a fat lot of good, then."

Lloyd shook his head. "It was more useful than you might think, actually. I looked up Tartessian. Apparently it's a script from the south of Portugal, so the next time I took some holiday I went there. I'd heard there was a big collection of inscriptions in Tartessian in a town called Almodôvar, so I went to check them out. It certainly looked like the same script, but I don't know why I thought I could work out an inscription that no-one else could read just by looking at old stones. It was when I was walking around the town that I found something." He took a sip of wine. Jocelyn had already drunk two glasses. Then, speaking quietly, he continued. "I found the bridge, Jocelyn – and the bank, though it didn't look quite like it does in The Dream. There's a little medieval bridge with three arches, and a raised grass bank on the other side, with some bushes. Here; take a look."

Lloyd passed over his phone. There were a lot of photos of the hump-backed bridge and a scrubby-looking bank. The position of the bridge and its distance from the raised bank were certainly right for what Jocelyn saw in the dream. But there were no trees, no cavities created by the roots, no flowers and, of course, no book.

Lloyd smiled. "I know. There might be a hundred places that look a bit like this. But finding it when I was on the trail of the letters? That seems like too much of a coincidence to me."

Jocelyn sat back. "So what do you think? Do we go to Portugal and start digging in that bank? I just want The Dream to stop, Lloyd. I've wanted it to stop for a long, long time. If someone, or something, is sending us the dream; if someone wants us to do something – fine! I'll do it. I'll do anything. I just want it to stop. Let's dig up the sodding bank."

He laughed. "It's pretty public, and I don't think the Portuguese authorities would appreciate that … Anyway, I'm not sure that's the point. Maybe the Almodôvar connection just tells us The Dream comes from somewhere. I've thought it was a message for a long time. I just don't know why it came to the three of us."

"So what have you done about it?" Jocelyn was becoming impatient with Lloyd's slow-burning approach to storytelling.

"I think it's pretty clear that someone wants us to find the book. But I've started to think we're looking for the book in the wrong place."

"You mean it's not in Portugal?"

"I mean it's not in the waking world."

"So it's just a dream? But you just said …"

"I said *waking* world, not *real* world. The dream *is* real, in its own way; I'm sure of that. I managed to get better at remembering the dream; that's how I wrote down those letters. And following those letters took me to a place that showed me the dream was real. But I've never – I've never been able to take control in the dream."

Jocelyn nodded. She had read enough books and websites about dreams to know what he meant. "It's never lucid. Not for me, either."

"I'm convinced that's the key. Making it a lucid dream; if we can control it, we can control how and when it ends. We can finally find out more about the book."

"So how do we do that? I've tried all the techniques to get more out of The Dream – the whole blue light thing, altering sleeping patterns, trying to catch yourself in REM sleep, memory techniques. Trust me, I've been there." Jocelyn assured him.

"I know a guy – he's a bit weird, but he's been helping me with this. I think we might be almost there. But having someone else who's had The Dream – well, that may be the breakthrough we're looking for. I'm seeing him tomorrow. Will you come?"

Jocelyn was very tempted. "I dunno … I have work tomorrow. And I need to get home to Laura."

"How old is she?"

"Seventeen."

"Is she OK to look after herself?"

"Sure, but …"

He moved his hand across the table towards her. "I think this is important, Jocelyn. It might not be a chance we get again. Text your daughter and tell her you'll be back tomorrow. I bet your work won't miss you."

"I sure as hell won't miss them." She hesitated; meeting Lloyd did seem too fortuitous for her to pass up the chance of sorting this out once and for all. It was worth a shot. "OK. I'll stay."

*

Jocelyn had drunk most of the rest of another bottle before they found their way to the Tube. When sober, Jocelyn very much doubted she would have agreed to stay the night at the home of a man she had last known nearly thirty years ago. But what she felt for Lloyd was akin to the sympathy a patient feels for a fellow sufferer of their disease – although Lloyd had not, it seemed, suffered from The Dream as much as she had. She drifted to sleep on the Tube; Lloyd nudged her awake when they got to Bermondsey. His flat was not far away, and Jocelyn soon found herself being introduced to Laurence, who came to the door in a red silk dressing gown.

"I found her! I found Jocelyn. How about that as a turn up for the books?"

Laurence gaped at her. "You're Jocelyn? Really?"

She laughed. "I see I'm pretty famous around here! I still don't know how Lloyd even recognised me. I sure as hell didn't recognise him."

Lloyd hung up his hat on a peg by the door.

"Oh, I think you would have done eventually. Can I get you another drink?"

Jocelyn knew it was not a good idea, but found herself saying yes anyway. Laurence threw open an impressive drinks cabinet and the three of them collapsed on a lavish three-piece suite.

"A shame you couldn't bump into Ryan too. Then you would have had all three of us!" Jocelyn commented as she took a sip of Bourbon. She was met by an awkward silence. Lloyd looked at his shoes.

"I'm really sorry, Jocelyn. I wasn't sure whether you knew or not."

"Sorry about what? Knew what?"

"Ryan died. In a car crash. What was it? Six years ago now, I think." Lloyd was rubbing his hands nervously.

Jocelyn thought the news should please her. Instead she felt buried by a weight of futility. It was not that she felt sorry for Ryan; it was just such a pathetic ending – and, of course, it robbed her of the chance to exact various baroque revenges she had been dreaming up over the years. She had to acknowledge she would have preferred the man alive rather than dead; and perhaps that was the closest to grieving for him she would ever come. But she was angry with Lloyd.

"You might have cared to mention this information when I was telling you about my history with Ryan."

"I wasn't sure whether you knew or not; and I didn't want to say ..."

Jocelyn thought about leaving there and then. Something about Lloyd's behaviour made her feel like he was treating her like a child. But it was nearly midnight; she would be on the train all night, or miss the last one, if she tried to get to King's Cross now. It made more sense to sleep on the situation and see how she felt in the morning.

*

Jocelyn awoke with an intense hangover. Laurence was already in the kitchen, and thrust a large cup of air-pressed coffee into her hand. In the grey dawning light she realised the true size of Lloyd's studio apartment, which overlooked the brown, pulsing Thames; over to the west, she could just see Tower Bridge and the grim bulk of the Tower of London behind it.

"I'm sorry about Lloyd last night," Laurence said, "You were quite right to be upset. Lloyd isn't always … the most tactful."

Although her head was throbbing, Jocelyn felt well-disposed towards Laurence for the coffee and the honesty. "That's sweet of you to say so."

"You've probably guessed that he's told me all about you – or at least what you went through as children. He tried to find you, you know."

"God, that sounds a bit stalkerish …" Jocelyn sat down at the breakfast bar, and cast her eyes over the tugs and barges that were beginning to drift past the window.

"When Ryan died, because Lloyd hadn't made contact with him before it happened, Lloyd got a bit desperate. He was worried that without the three of you …"

"He thought he needed all three of us to get rid of The Dream."

Laurence nodded. "He thought he might need all of you, yes. Obviously that's not an option now, but Lloyd's found this guy, Karim, who thinks he can do things with dreams. I mean, living with Lloyd has made me pretty open-minded about weird stuff with dreams, but I'm not sure about Karim. It was Karim who said they really needed you to unlock the dream. He even said he could get hold of you. That was just two days ago."

"You mean he can track people down?"

"Not in the usual way, no. Or so he claims. He said he could make Lloyd bump into you."

It was too early in the morning, and Jocelyn was too hung over, to process this. "So we're off to see some kind of wizard?" She felt as though she had blundered into some alternative reality. But in her actual reality she still needed to call into work sick and check on Laura. She greeted Lloyd rather coolly when he finally emerged, but Jocelyn had already decided to go ahead and meet Karim. At this point, things could hardly get any weirder.

*

Karim lived at the top of one of those huge Victorian houses in Hackney that had been artists' squats in the '80s, with a basement overgrown with freakishly tall and vibrant weeds and alarmingly steep front steps. His flat was strikingly Spartan, to the extent that Jocelyn wondered where he kept the necessities of London life; he ushered them into a living room containing little more than three cushions on the floor. Karim was younger than Jocelyn expected; he dressed in an unbleached linen robe, consistent with his minimalist décor, and spoke with theatrical slowness; Jocelyn thought she detected a trace of a French accent.

"Welcome, Jocelyn."

She struggled to suppress a smile when Lloyd actually bowed to their host; as she expected, Karim immediately claimed credit for Lloyd meeting her in Treadwells.

"I told you I could find Jocelyn for you; and here she is. You don't seem convinced, Jocelyn?" He fixed her with a stare that was undeniably unnerving. "You're quite right, of course. It's up to me to convince you. Sit."

The large cushions in the middle of the floor were surprisingly comfortable.

"Has Lloyd explained to you what I propose to do?"

Lloyd threw up his hands. "I haven't said anything, really …"

Karim nodded slowly. "Until you can gain lucidity in The Dream, it will be impossible for either of you to move forward, either in The Dream or in your lives. Having you here, Jocelyn, increases the chances that one or other of you will be able to attain lucidity. I hope you both manage it, but there are no guarantees."

"And what's the point, exactly? What's the point of knowing I'm dreaming?" Jocelyn asked.

Karim pursed his lips and closed his eyes, ostentatiously weighing his answer. "That is the basic meaning of lucidity, yes. But you will need to go beyond just being aware you are dreaming. The Dream always ends as soon as you pick up the book, yes? You will need to hold on to The Dream, to see it through; and you will need to act intentionally. The only way to escape The Dream is to respond to its message; and that requires you to see The Dream through to the finish. There may be signs in The Dream you will only see if you change how you act. Are there other people there? Are there other books? You can only know if you gain control of your astral body in The Dream."

Outside, beyond a threadbare net curtain, it was beginning to rain on a glimpse of slate roofs, skylights and dormer windows. Karim's room was so simple he did not even have a lampshade on the single glaring light bulb that illuminated it, but there was something studied about this simplicity – as if Karim were engaged in some sort of performance. Jocelyn, like Laurence, did not trust Karim; but she was not sure what he wanted out of this. Certainly she had no intention of parting with any money – nor could she afford to.

"I suppose this will cost me something? I can't afford to pay you, I'm afraid."

Karim smiled lightly. "I don't do this for payment, Jocelyn. I am an explorer of dreams. You and Lloyd are dreamers of a unique dream. Working with you – well, it's like being invited to climb an untouched mountain. This is worth doing, in and of itself."

Jocelyn was unconvinced. But she had always been impressed by coincidences; perhaps it was the cumulative effect of The Dream itself, filling her life with unfulfilled and unexplained enchantment. And the coincidence of meeting Lloyd was still too good to pass up if it meant being free of The Dream – even if Karim had to be involved.

She looked at Karim. "OK. Tell me what I have to do."

*

As if responding to all the renewed attention it was receiving, The Dream began to recur weekly, with both Jocelyn and Lloyd dreaming it at the same time. They agreed to text one another first thing in the morning, as soon as it occurred. After Lloyd offered to pay her train fare, Jocelyn met with Lloyd and Karim every Saturday; and there, in Karim's bare flat, he attempted to help them recover as much of The Dream as possible. Jocelyn pretended to her daughter she had started a training course in London; she had never dared tell Laura about The Dream.

Karim assured them they would find it progressively easier to remember details of The Dream; and as their recall improved, they would find themselves on the threshold of lucid dreaming. At first, Jocelyn was contemptuous of Karim's technique, which involved intense meditative visualization and questioning on details of The Dream. It seemed to be making no difference whatsoever. But after a few weeks, Lloyd announced that a breakthrough had come; just as he was walking down from the bridge towards the bank, Lloyd managed to turn his head to look at the river.

"But I was dreaming at the same time – " Jocelyn objected, "and I didn't look at the river. So we're no longer dreaming the same dream; we're no longer the same dreamer. How does that work?"

Karim waited a long time before answering.

"You ask a very good question, Jocelyn. I am not sure I know the answer. But yes, as each of you develops lucidity you become different dreamers; that is certainly true."

Jocelyn began to notice something different about The Dream two weeks later; as she crossed the bridge, she seemed to see a hazy, attenuated human figure step out of her own body and advance before her towards the bank. Karim smiled broadly when she mentioned it.

"You saw your fellow dreamer; it was you, Lloyd, walking faster than Jocelyn."

Lloyd glanced nervously towards Jocelyn.

"So I'm still stuck at the original pace?" She asked.

"So it seems; but lucidity will come."

Lucidity was certainly taking its sweet time to arrive, Jocelyn thought. As the weeks passed, she seemed to become a passive watcher in The Dream, observing an increasingly clear figure of Lloyd taking her place and advancing towards the book. Lloyd had begun prolonging The Dream, too – opening the book, and even managing to recall some of the symbols and images within it; but for Jocelyn, The Dream still ended as soon as Lloyd opened the book. She also noticed how interested Karim was in those early, tentative scribbles of the interior of the book. He took Lloyd's notes, and declared he needed to keep them.

"It's best for you not to have these. They will be imperfect, and they will prejudice your memory when trying to transcribe them again."

Jocelyn was sure she detected glee in Karim's studiedly impassive face. This was what he wanted out of this; this was why he was pretending to help them. Karim wanted to know what was inside the book. One Saturday, as she and Lloyd picked their way down the mossy steps of Karim's house into the spring sunshine, Jocelyn raised it with Lloyd. He laughed off the idea.

"It's not as though he can even read the symbols; I mean, I'm hardly a reliable conduit to secret knowledge, even if you think that stuff means anything at all."

"Karim thinks it does. I can feel it. Lloyd, I think he's using us. Using you to read the book, while I – well, I suppose I'm some sort of experimental control, aren't I? I just stand there and look."

They found a small Iranian café and ordered espressos. Jocelyn was determined to get through to Lloyd that she thought this was a dangerous situation for them to be in.

"He's got inside our heads now, Lloyd. I'll be honest – I don't know what he's trying to do, exactly. But I don't like it. And I'm afraid … well, I'm afraid I'm out."

Lloyd jerked upright in his seat.

"You're out? Joss – you can't…"

She shook her head. "It's not like you need me anyway. What am I really doing?"

"But it's part – "

She cut him off. "Part of Karim's plan. Yeah. That's my point."

Lloyd seemed deflated by her decision, but Jocelyn knew she needed to stand firm. It was not as though she was likely to stop dreaming The Dream any time soon; but she could not be part of Karim's experiments. Lloyd must have told Karim, because he tried to call her a dozen times on her journey back. She blocked his number and deleted it from her phone. The more time she spent thinking about it, the more she realised that getting Karim involved had been a stupid mistake, and one whose consequences she had only just escaped.

*

Jocelyn was used to the new pattern of The Dream by now. She was walking over the bridge; then, a moment later, she came to a halt and the rest of The Dream was merely witnessed; she saw Lloyd's back as he strode down the hump of the bridge and went towards the bank. He spent a few moments looking for the book; then he knelt down, reverently retrieved the book and held it in his hands. This was where The Dream ended for her, and she had no idea how much of the book Lloyd was able to read now. He had clearly been hurt by her decision to pull out of the experiments, and she got no replies to her texts. But she needed to know he was safe. Eventually, it occurred to her to make contact with Laurence instead. She soon found him on Facebook. Laurence was only too glad to tell her he was worried about how much time Lloyd was spending with Karim. He rang Jocelyn from work.

"I think you need to do something, Jocelyn."

"I've told you, he won't get back to me. I can't do anything. That's why I wanted you to ask him to speak to me."

"I don't mean that. I mean you need to do something – in The Dream."

Jocelyn was silent for a moment. "I can't do anything in The Dream. All I do now is watch Lloyd."

"You paused. I could tell you were thinking about it. I think you can do it, Jocelyn."

"Do what? Even if I could move – what could I do?"

"There's a book. There's a river. And I'm damned if Karim's going to turn Lloyd into some sort of dictating machine for whatever he wants from that book. You need to get rid of the book, Jocelyn – get rid of it in The Dream."

Afterwards, Jocelyn thought for a long time about what Laurence had said. It made a certain amount of sense, if only she could get herself moving. But weeks of practice had not brought true lucidity. She went over everything in her mind: the return of The Dream after so long; going to London; meeting Lloyd in Treadwells; learning about Ryan; meeting Karim; breaking off the experiments. There was something missing – some element she was ignoring. A few days after speaking to Laurence she realised, with a shudder, what that element might be.

Perhaps, after all, there was a third dreamer.

The thought filled her with a mixture of disgust and fear; but she had to broach it with Laurence.

"What about Ryan? Do dead people still dream?"

"Damn, Jocelyn – I didn't see that one coming. No-one knows, do they?"

"But he might still be there. And I have a feeling – a sort of feeling that he is. Or at least a feeling that something's missing, and I think it's him."

"Christ, well … I suppose that changes things. Let me go away and think about it. I might know someone."

Laurence and Jocelyn arranged to meet in London. Lloyd, of course, was with Karim at the time.

"There's someone I used to know at university," Laurence explained, as the pigeons milled around them. "She's a bit weird – well, as you'd expect, I suppose. But she thinks she can talk to dead people."

Jocelyn covered her face. "Oh God – not the Spiritualists, please!"

"I can't say she really does, of course. But I can say she's not one of those charlatans, because she doesn't like doing it. She sure as hell doesn't charge people money for it. But there were things that happened when we were at Cambridge – things I can't really explain any other way. All I can do is ask her to talk to Ryan. And I can't promise she'll say yes. It's pretty likely, actually, that she'll say no." He threw up his hands. "But it's there. You can try it if you want. Up to you."

"How worried are you, Laurence."

He smiled weakly. "I'm scared. I'm scared Lloyd is slipping away. I can't get through to him anymore. He sits there for hours now, Jocelyn – in the early morning, writing it all down in a notebook for Karim. It all goes to Karim. Lloyd's not eating properly, either. You should look at him; it's like he's aged a decade."

Jocelyn felt for Laurence; and it was out of compassion for him, she told herself, that she agreed to meet with Laurence's friend Selina at Laurence and Lloyd's flat (Lloyd, once more, was with Karim). Selina was small, agitated, angry, and unwilling to take off her scarf indoors, which half hid her face. She regarded Jocelyn with unconcealed hostility.

"I'm doing this for Laurence." She declared. "I owe him a favour. I honestly don't care who you are, or what your problem is. Have you got it?"

She held out a hand. Selina had asked Jocelyn to bring an object that once belonged to Ryan. It had not been easy to find one; Jocelyn had long since thrown away every gift he ever gave her, along with all the letters he wrote. Eventually she remembered a cold night in Leicester (where Ryan was at university) when he lent her a bottle-green rugby shirt to wear. She remembered she was still wearing it on the train home, and how silly she felt in a man's rugby shirt, and she was fairly certain she never returned it. But the chances that it was still at the house where she grew up were slim. Jocelyn arranged a weekend visit to her father, in which she searched for the shirt under the pretext of cleaning and tidying the house. She was astonished when she actually found it – faded, stained, stuffed under the sink and repurposed as a cleaning cloth. She felt embarrassed as she handed over the ruined shirt to Selina.

"Here."

"And you're sure this was his?"

"Yeah. It's his shirt. Although my dad's been using it as a cleaning rag for the last twenty years."

"And he gave it to you?"

Jocelyn nodded.

"That's good. It means there's a connection to him and a connection to you." She pushed the shirt into a capacious carpetbag she was carrying. "I'll see what happens."

That was it. Jocelyn had been expecting some explanation of what Selina might do. "She says they come to her," Laurence said, after the door shut on Selina. "She can't predict when they'll come, or if they'll come, but she can speak to them. Apparently it helps to have something a person owned."

"She's a sunny personality, isn't she?"

"She hates it. It's a curse, not a gift."

And so the waiting began. Jocelyn was not even sure how she would know if Selina had talked to Ryan; and she was far from certain that she believed such a thing was possible. But her life had now become so strange that she had arrived at a resigned acceptance of the strange.

*

Every time, she wished she could reach out and stop Lloyd as he strode ahead of her on the bridge. All he was now was a drone, programmed to do Karim's bidding and recover more and more of the book. Jocelyn had no idea how much of the book Lloyd had managed to transcribe for Karim, or what Karim planned to do with it – but she knew now that she had to stop Lloyd reading that book, and if that meant destroying it then that was a price worth paying – especially if it meant ending The Dream forever and removing this blight on Jocelyn's life. Yet, try as she might, Jocelyn was rooted to the spot – in that terrifying paralysis that so often weighs down the dreamer at the very threshold of lucidity, but unable to left their foot to cross it.

Someone else did take action. A few nights after her meeting with Selina, Jocelyn was surprised to hear Selina's voice on the phone.

"I thought you needed to know. Laurence was arrested."

"Arrested? What! By the police?" Jocelyn's first, terrified thought was that Laurence had tried to harm Karim in some way, or even Lloyd – although he hardly struck her as a violent man.

"For arson. The idiot tried to burn down someone's flat."

"In Hackney?"

"How did you know that? Christ, if you're involved in this …"

"It's alright – no, I'm not involved. I didn't know about it. I just guessed. I knew there was something – something Laurence really badly wanted destroyed. Do you know if he burnt the flat down?"

"Well the Fire Brigade got there pretty quickly; so no, he didn't burn it down. They flooded the place with water, of course."

Jocelyn was smiling. It sounded as though Laurence had done it. Karim would be furious.

"The guy who lived there – he was OK, right?"

"There was nobody there at the time, apparently."

Jocelyn sighed with relief. "Thanks for telling me. I really appreciate it. I wanted to ask you – did you have any – ?"

But Selina put the phone down. Clearly she anticipated that Jocelyn was about to ask her about Ryan. That wait would have to continue. And if Laurence was in custody she had lost her last tenuous link with Lloyd in the waking world, even if she saw him every time The Dream returned.

Then, finally, something happened differently. The Dream came back about ten days after Jocelyn last spoke to Selina. It proceeded in the usual way; Lloyd was standing with his back to her, hunched intently over the open book; and as Jocelyn thought The Dream was about to end for her, a second figure emerged from behind the grassy bank. Unmistakably, it was Ryan; not the student she remembered, but an older man already well on the way to baldness. He was perfectly human, just as much as Lloyd; nothing about him was eldritch, deathly or macabre. Nothing suggested this man was no longer alive. But he was wearing a bottle-green shirt.

Ryan looked briefly in Jocelyn's direction. She thought he smiled slightly, although he was probably just registering her presence. It took a moment for Lloyd, absorbed in the book, to notice Ryan's approach. Clearly, he had not expected to be disturbed. Jocelyn was surprised that she was still in The Dream – it should have ended for her, by this point; and she wondered whether Ryan, somehow, was keeping her there to watch what happened next. Ryan laid his hands on the book, and Lloyd pulled it back protectively. The two men were soon tussling over it, but Ryan eventually wrested it out of Lloyd's hands without too much difficulty. Then, to Jocelyn's astonishment, Ryan was coming towards her with the book. He stopped at a discreet distance and held it out to her.

"You can take it. Just reach out."

She could; as soon as he said the words, she had the power of independent movement; for the first time ever, she was neither an automaton moved by the direction of The Dream, nor a paralysed watcher rooted to the spot.

Slowly, tentatively, she reached out to take the book. Lloyd, she could see, was sitting on the bank in despair, his head in his hands.

For a moment she was tempted to open it. At last she had the power to do so; to see what lay within. She squeezed the book's leather gently, studying its beautiful cover. But that was not why she was here. Jocelyn smiled at Ryan, turned towards the river and pitched the book over the bridge's parapet into the waters below. She had made her choice.

As if dissolving in a smudge of ink, The Dream vanished. Jocelyn was awake at home. Some blue light was coming through the curtains. She knew it was the end of The Dream; not just the end of The Dream that night, or the end of The Dream for her. It was over. She felt the weight lifted. The Dream sought a response and she had finally given one, even if it was an answer she never thought she would have the strength to give.

Jocelyn's phone was ringing. After all these months, it was Lloyd. She picked it up.

"So it did need all three of us, after all," she said.

ALSO PUBLISHED BY ST JURMIN PRESS

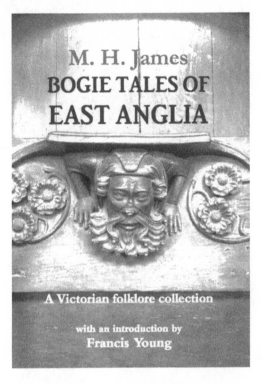

Originally published in 1891, *Bogie Tales of East Anglia* by Margaret Helen James was the first book devoted to the folklore of East Anglia. However, the book vanished into obscurity soon after publication, and has never been reprinted until now. Featuring witchcraft, ghosts, charms, traditional cures, legendary tales and an assortment of terrifying spectres (including East Anglia's demon dog, Black Shuck), Margaret James's book is an important source for the folklore current in the Waveney Valley and Suffolk coast in the late 19th century. This critical edition, with an introduction and detailed notes by the folklorist Francis Young, makes available for the first time a rare and elusive book on the supernatural folklore of Norfolk and Suffolk.

ISBN 9780992640460
126pp.
Available from lulu.com

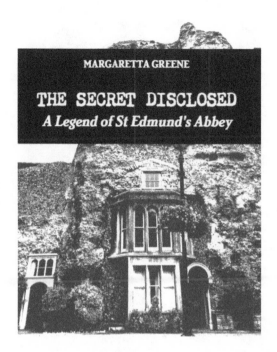

MARGARETTA GREENE

THE SECRET DISCLOSED
A Legend of St Edmund's Abbey

In 1860, 23 year-old Margaretta Greene was inspired by unexplained phenomena in her family home (which was built into the ruins of the Abbey of Bury St Edmunds) to write a historical novella which gave a narrative to Bury St Edmunds' best-known ghost, the infamous 'Grey Lady' who haunts the ruins of St Edmunds Abbey. Greene told the story of Maude Carew, a nun whose desperate love for a monk of St Edmunds Abbey leads her to conspire with Queen Margaret of Anjou and murder King Henry VI's uncle, Humphrey Duke of Gloucester. The novella proved so sensational in Victorian Bury that it even provoked a riot, but until now it has never been republished and has remained a scarce and elusive work. This edition reprints the original text of Greene's novella along with an extensive introduction by historian Francis Young. Fully referenced with an index and bibliography, this is an authoritative study of Greene's novella as well as an edition of the text.

ISBN 9780992640477
88pp., black and white illustrations
Available from lulu.com

CPSIA information can be obtained
at www.ICGtesting.com
Printed in the USA
BVHW030215300321
603700BV00007B/260